W9-AMB-687

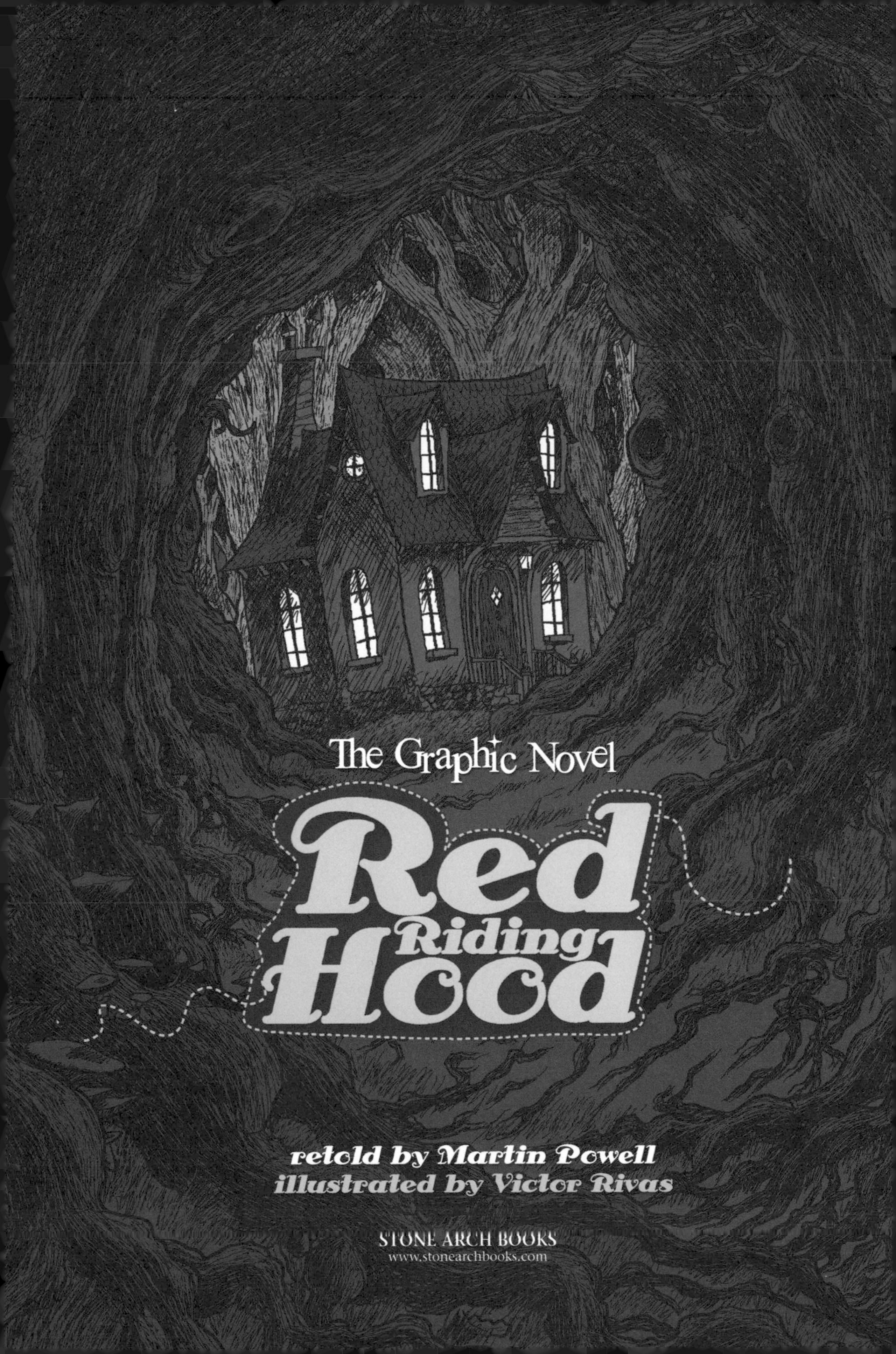

The Graphic Novel

# Red Riding Hood

retold by Martin Powell
illustrated by Victor Rivas

STONE ARCH BOOKS
www.stonearchbooks.com

Graphic Spin is published by Stone Arch Books
151 Good Counsel Drive, P.O. Box 669
Mankato, Minnesota 56002
*www.stonearchbooks.com*

*Library of Congress Cataloging-in-Publication Data*
Powell, Martin.
  Red Riding Hood: The Graphic Novel / retold by Martin Powell; illustrated by Victor Rivas.
  p. cm. — (Graphic Spin)
  ISBN 978-1-4342-0769-2 (library binding)
  ISBN 978-1-4342-0865-1 (pbk.)
  1. Graphic novels. [1. Graphic novels.] I. Rivas, Victor, ill. II. Little Red Riding Hood. English.
III. Title.
PZ7.7.P69Red 2009
[Fic]—dc22                                                              2008006723

Summary: One morning, young Ruby sets out to visit her grandma's house. She wears a red riding
hood to protect her from the forest's evil creatures. But will it? A hungry, old wolf has some evil plans
of his own.

Art Director: Heather Kindseth
Graphic Designer: Kay Fraser

**Librarian Reviewer**
Katharine Kan
Graphic novel reviewer and Library Consultant, Panama City, FL
MLS in Library and Information Studies, University of Hawaii at Manoa, HI

**Reading Consultant**
Elizabeth Stedem
Educator/Consultant, Colorado Springs, CO
MA in Elementary Education, University of Denver, CO

1 2 3 4 5 6 13 12 11 10 09 08

Printed in the United States of America

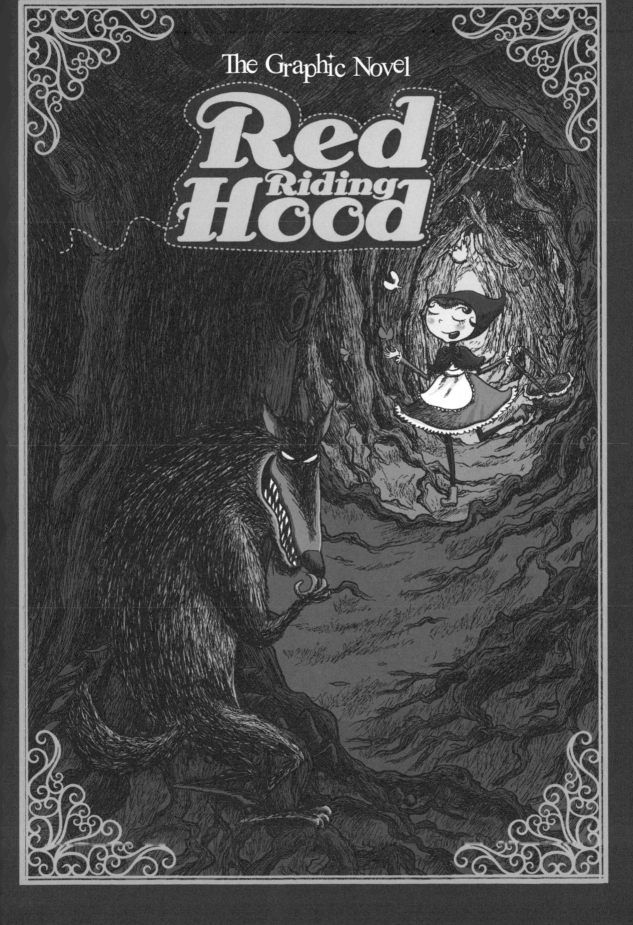

The Graphic Novel

# Red Riding Hood

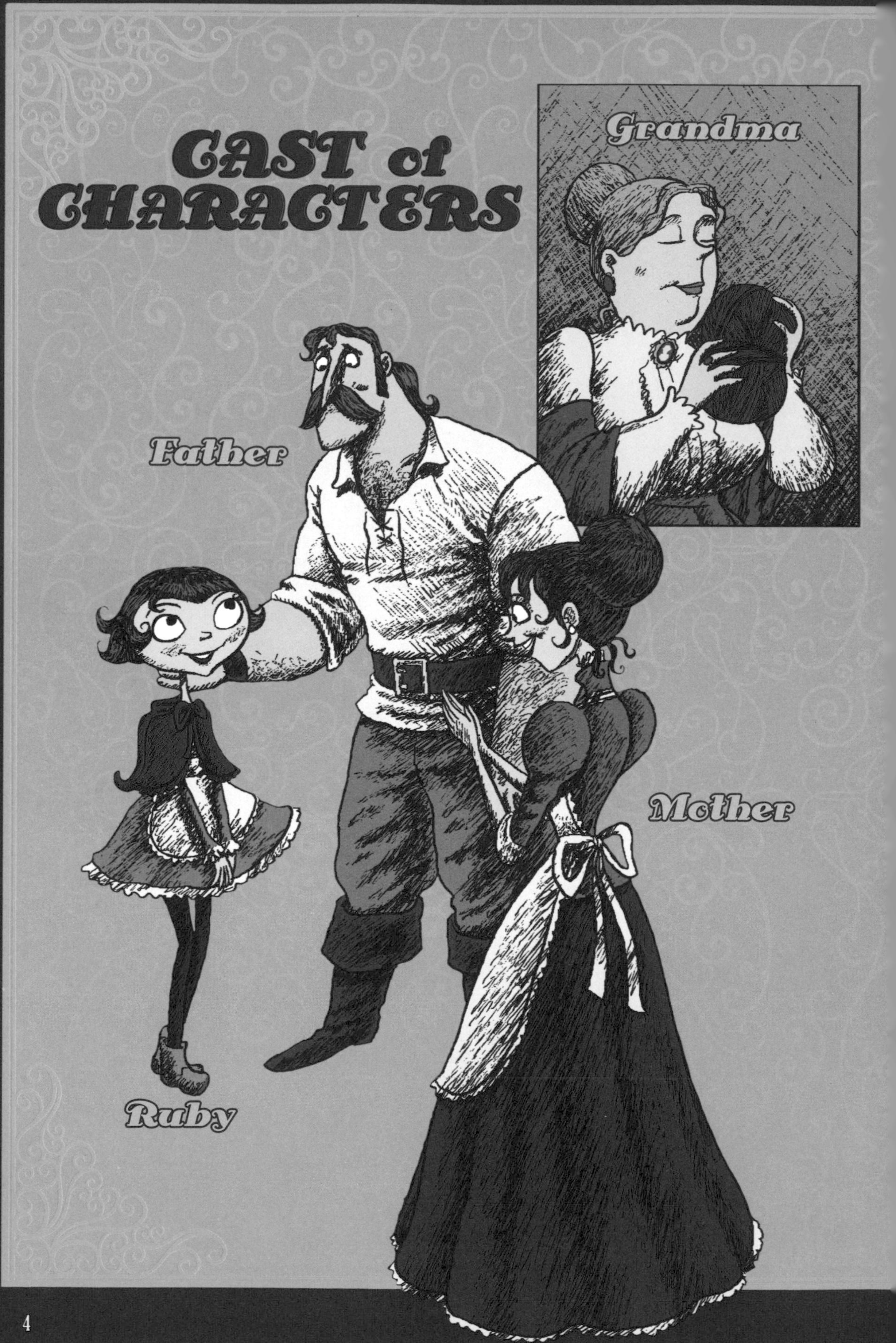
CAST of CHARACTERS
Grandma
Father
Mother
Ruby

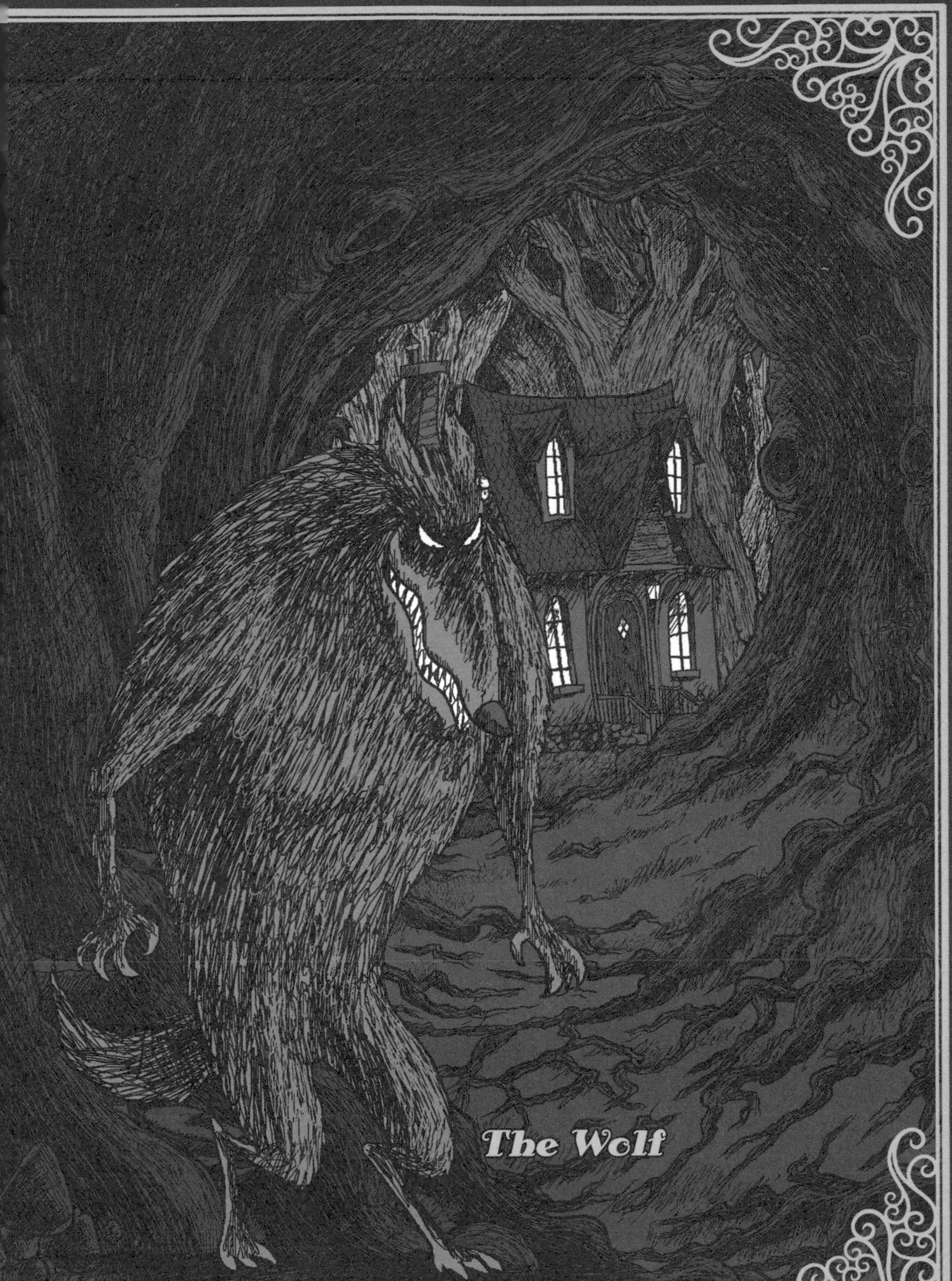
The Wolf

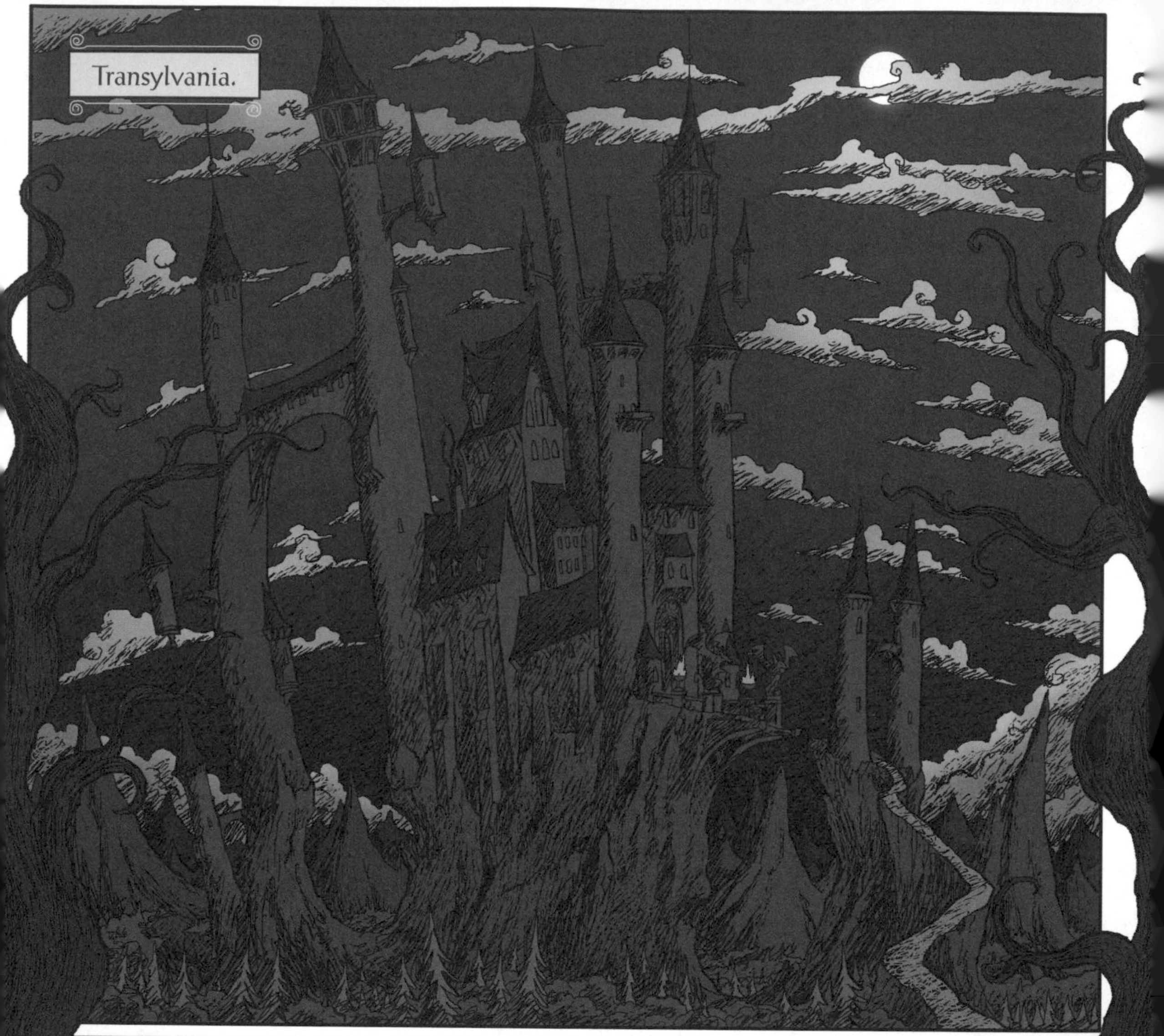
Transylvania.

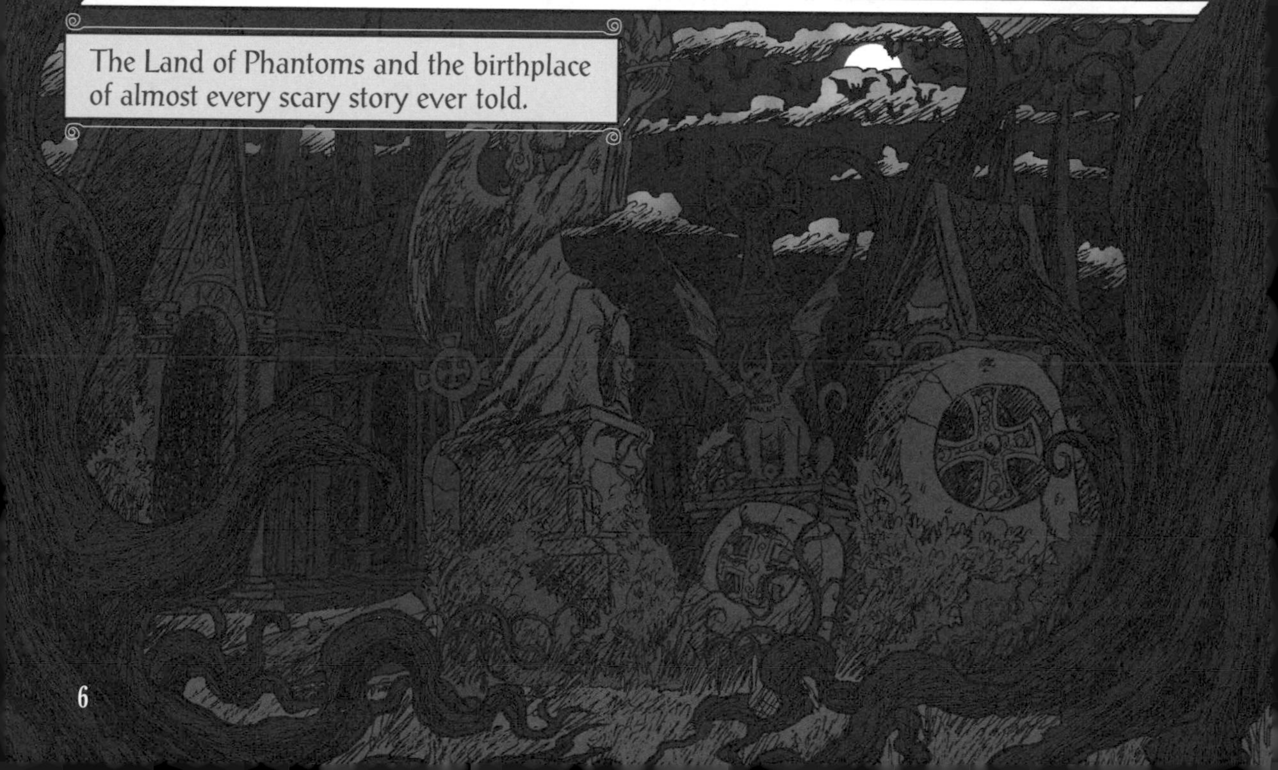
The Land of Phantoms and the birthplace of almost every scary story ever told.

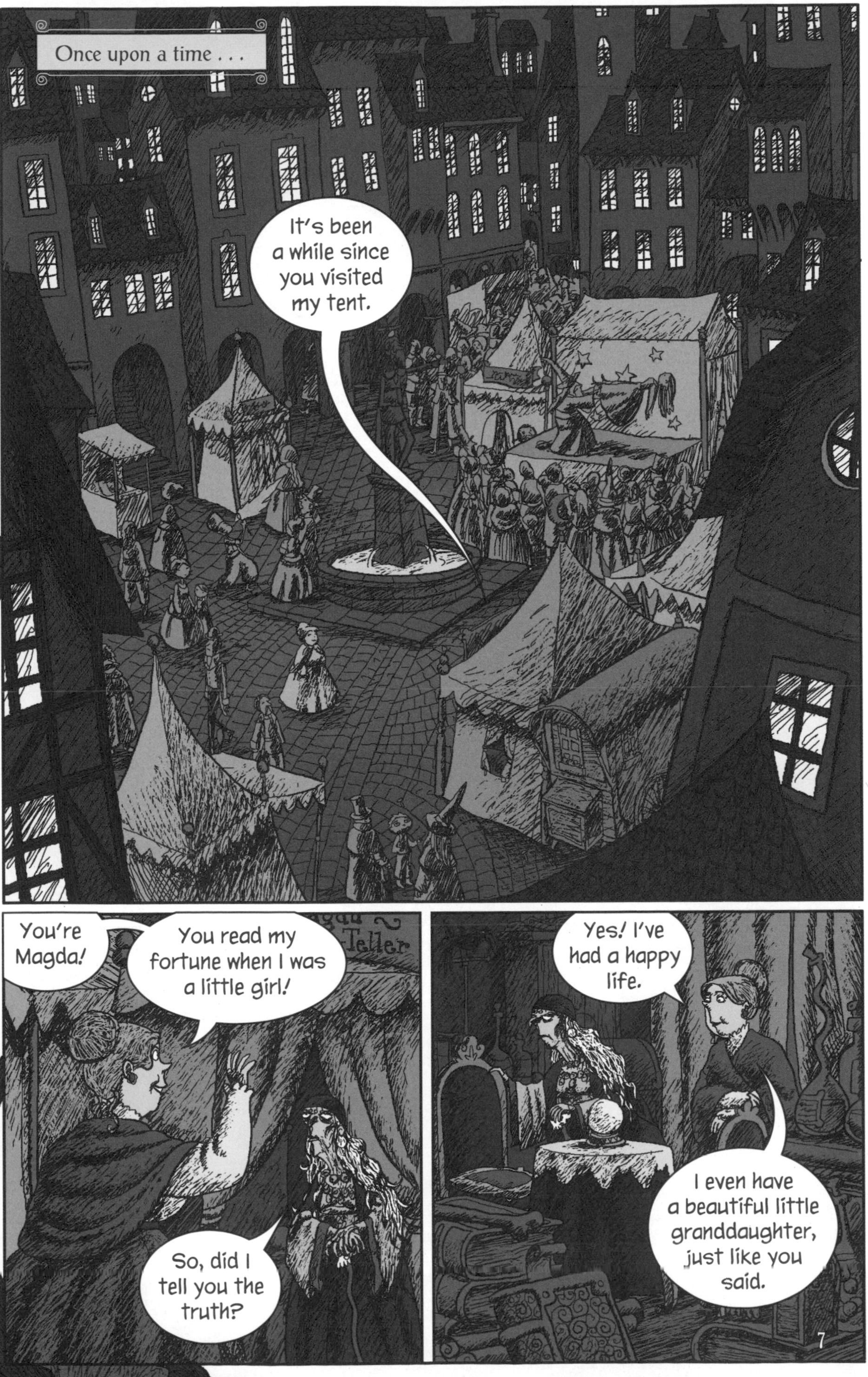
Once upon a time . . .
It's been a while since you visited my tent.
You're Magda!
You read my fortune when I was a little girl!
So, did I tell you the truth?
Yes! I've had a happy life.
I even have a beautiful little granddaughter, just like you said.

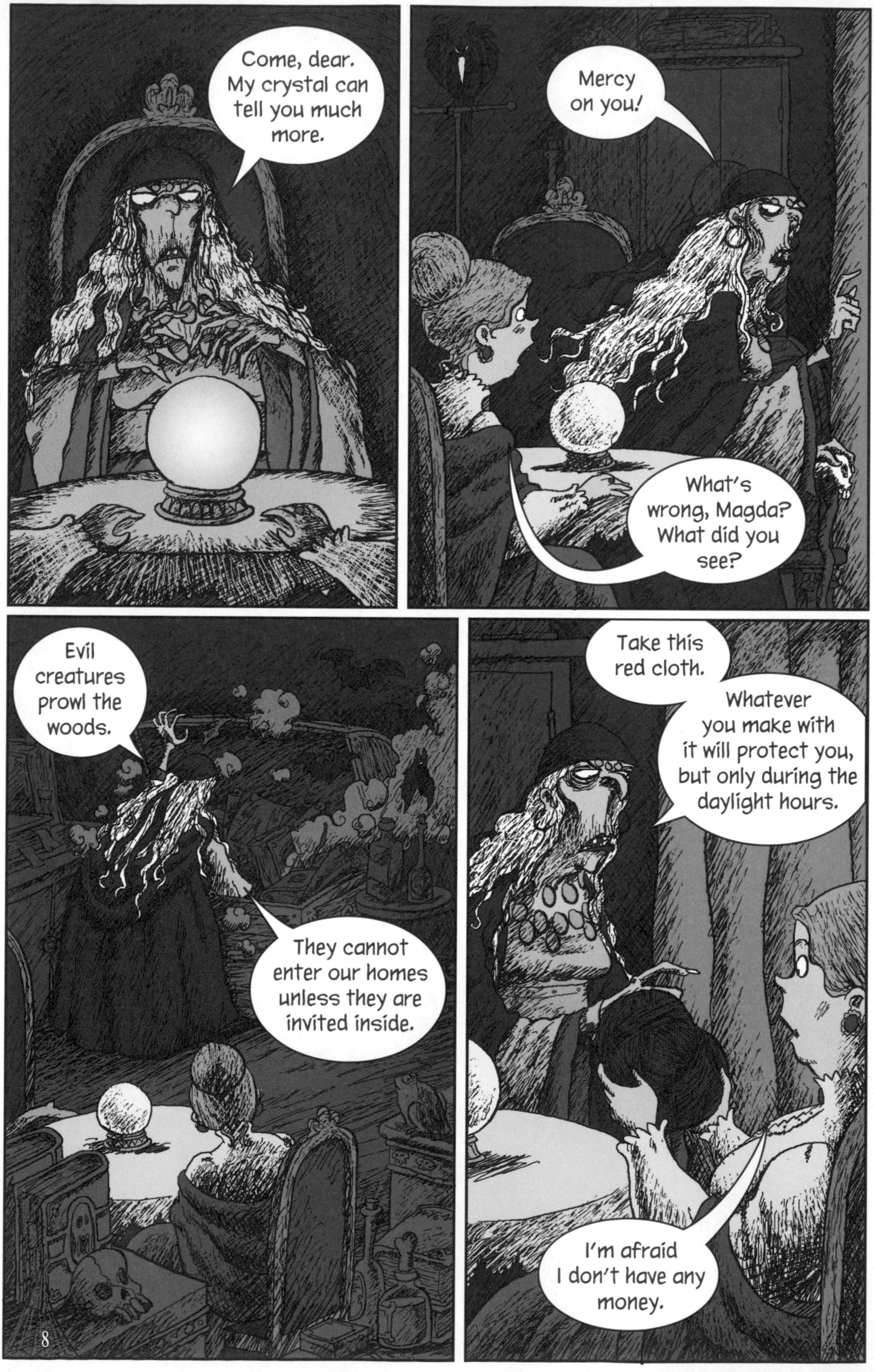
Come, dear. My crystal can tell you much more.
Mercy on you!
What's wrong, Magda? What did you see?
Evil creatures prowl the woods.
They cannot enter our homes unless they are invited inside.
Take this red cloth.
Whatever you make with it will protect you, but only during the daylight hours.
I'm afraid I don't have any money.

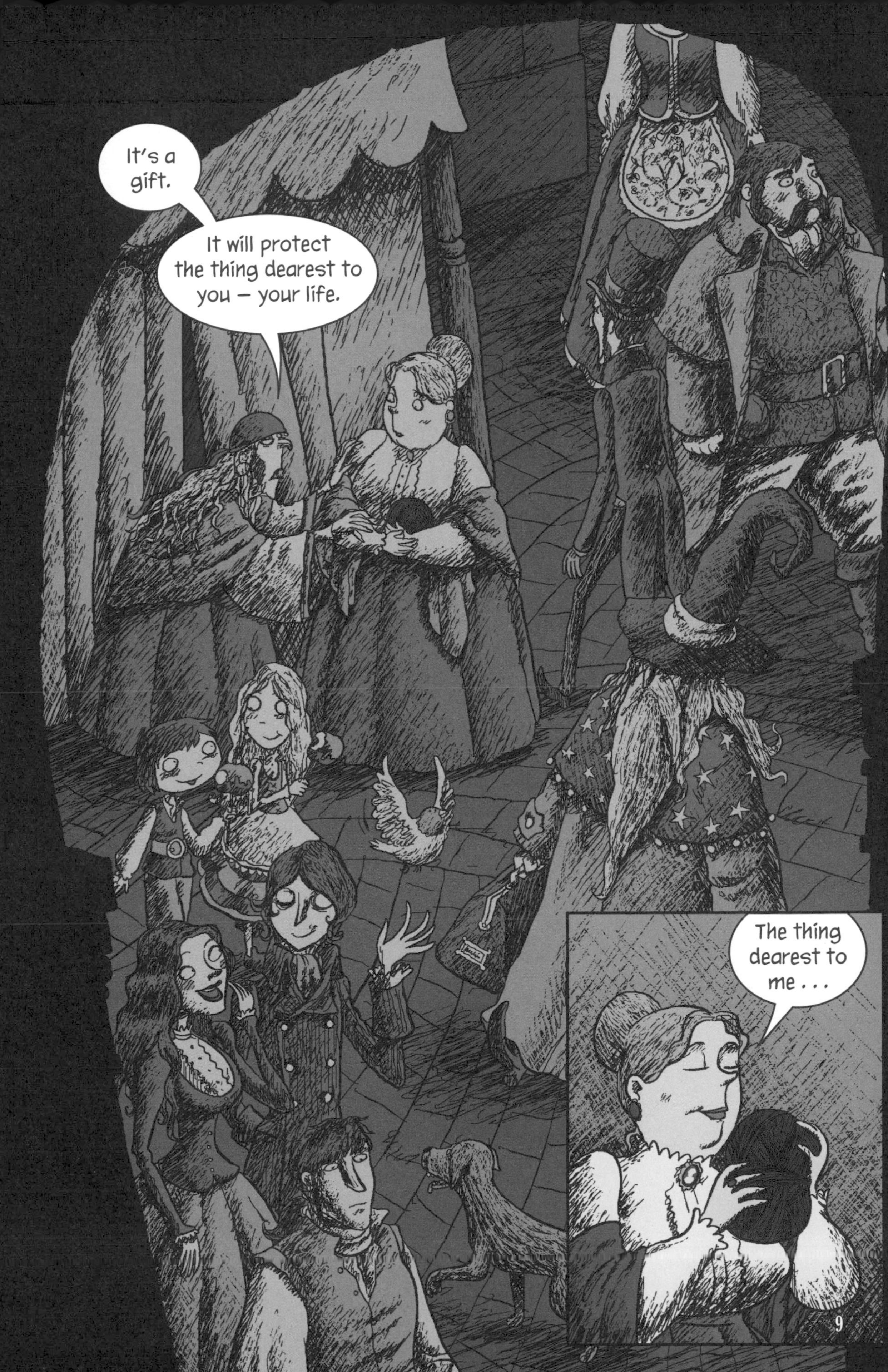
It's a gift.
It will protect the thing dearest to you – your life.
The thing dearest to me . . .

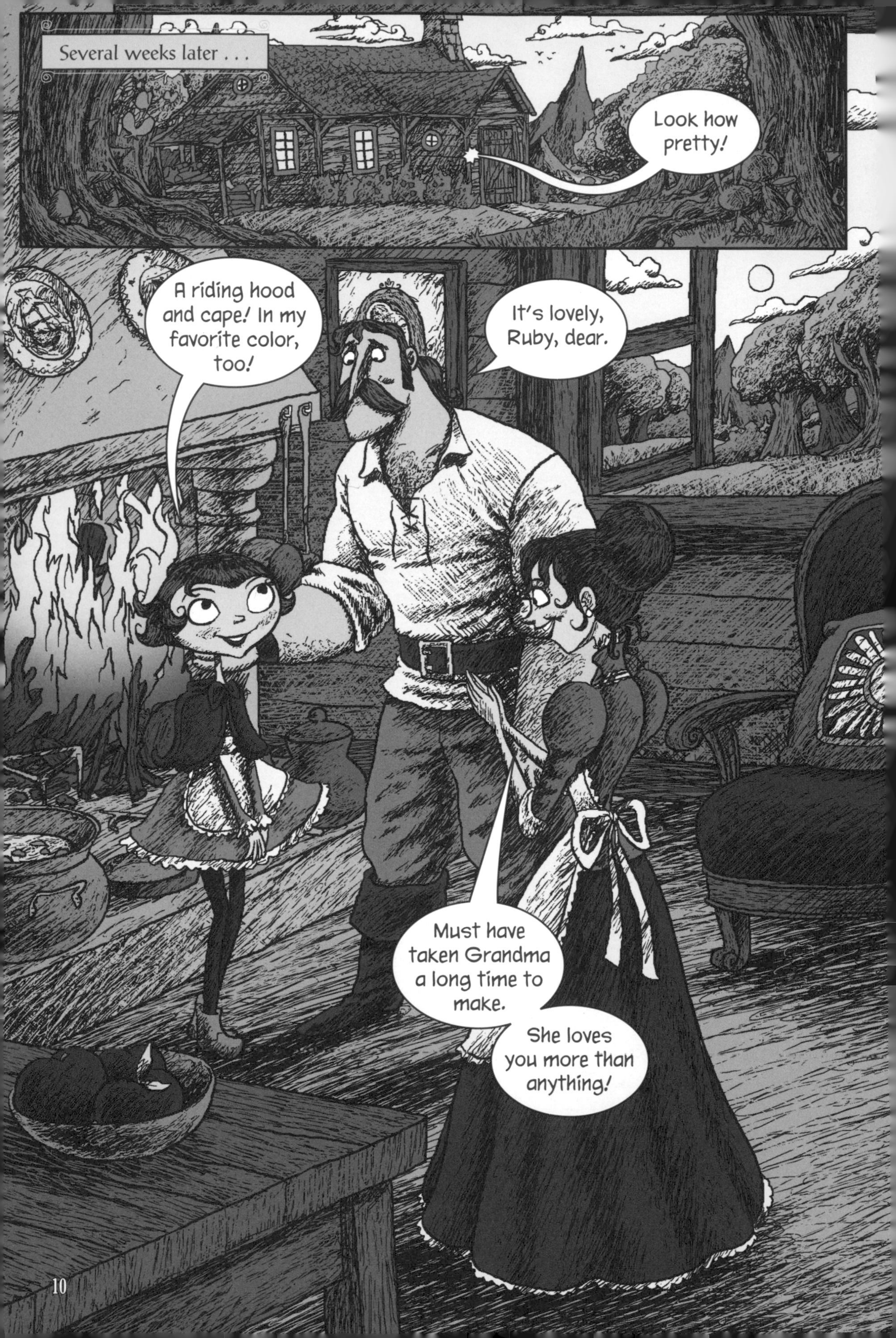
Several weeks later . . .
Look how pretty!
A riding hood and cape! In my favorite color, too!
It's lovely, Ruby, dear.
Must have taken Grandma a long time to make.
She loves you more than anything!

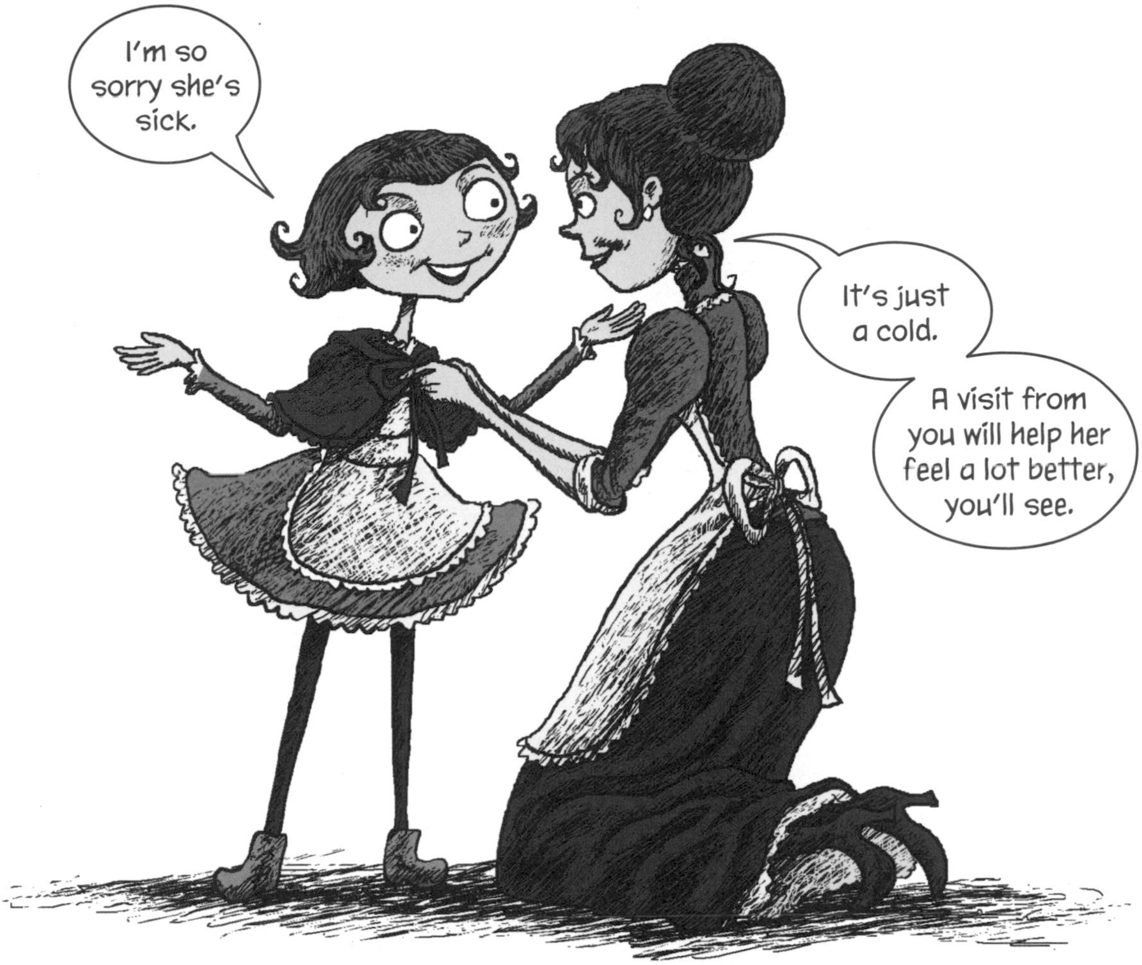
I'm so sorry she's sick.
It's just a cold.
A visit from you will help her feel a lot better, you'll see.

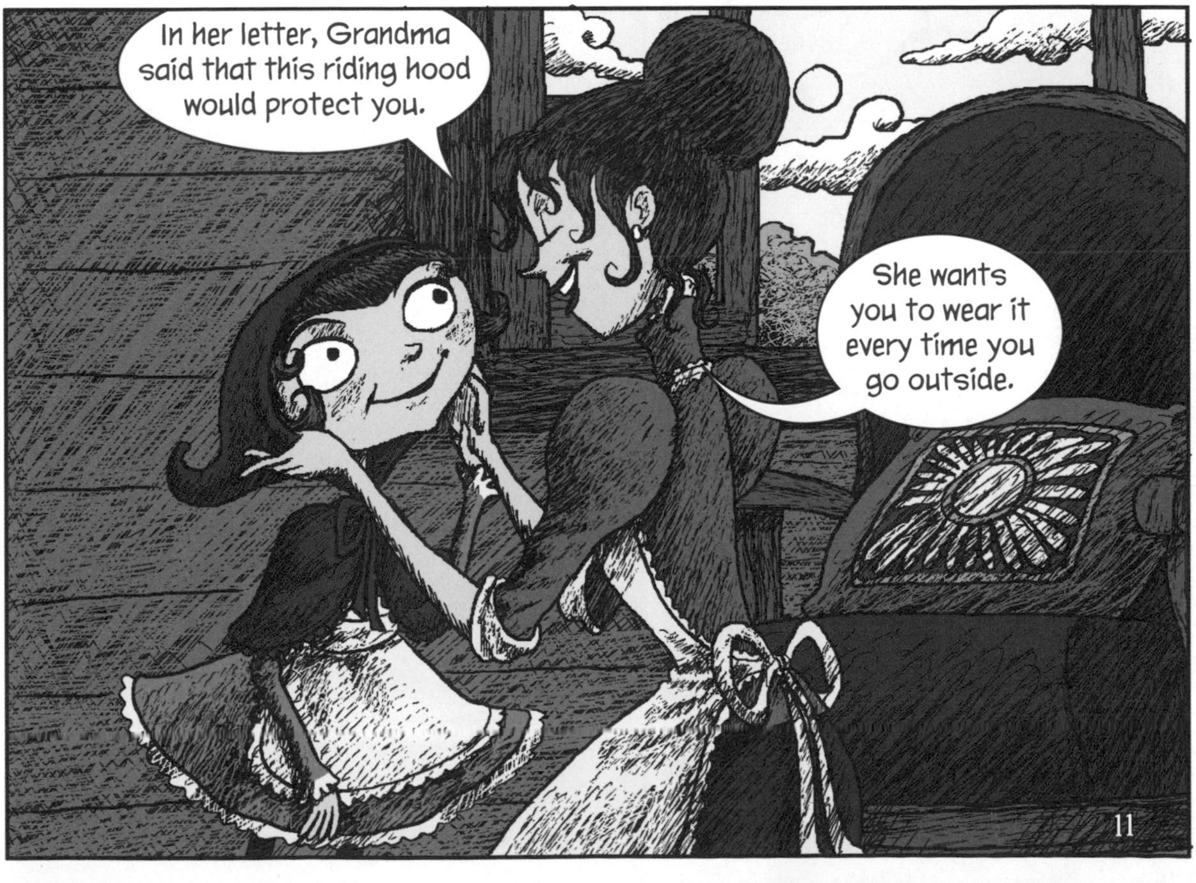
In her letter, Grandma said that this riding hood would protect you.
She wants you to wear it every time you go outside.

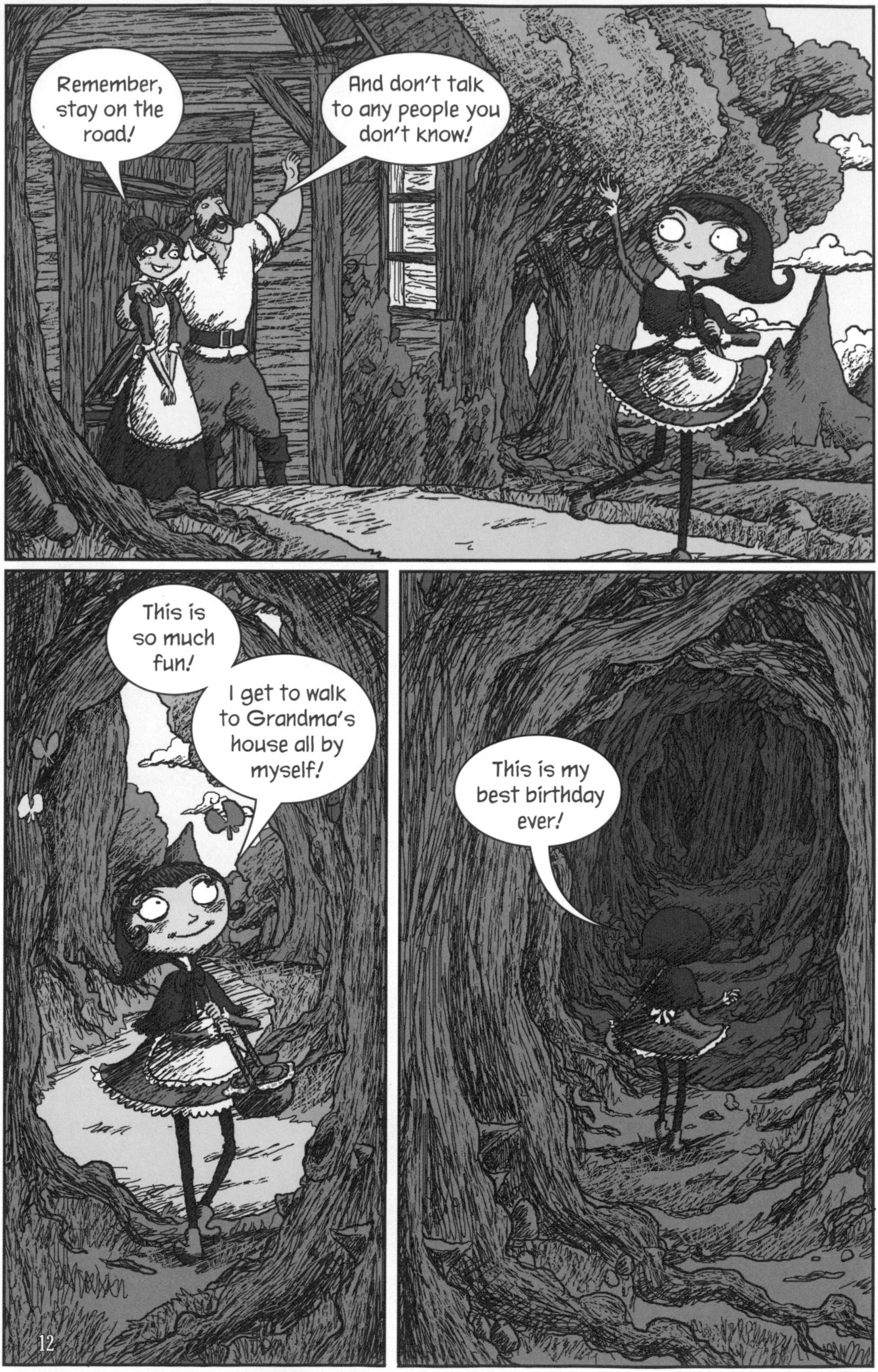
Remember, stay on the road!
And don't talk to any people you don't know!
This is so much fun!
I get to walk to Grandma's house all by myself!
This is my best birthday ever!

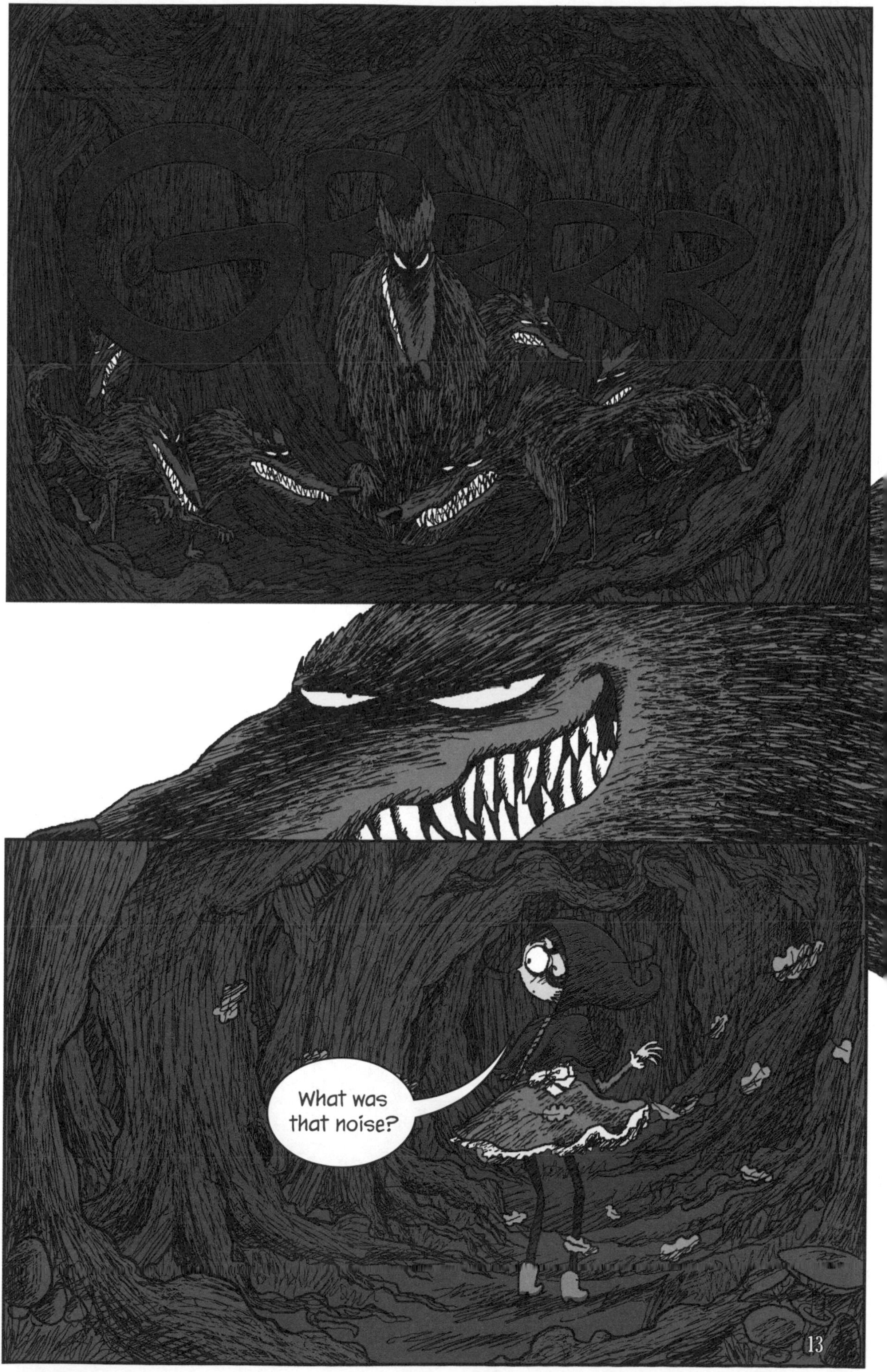
GRRRR
What was that noise?

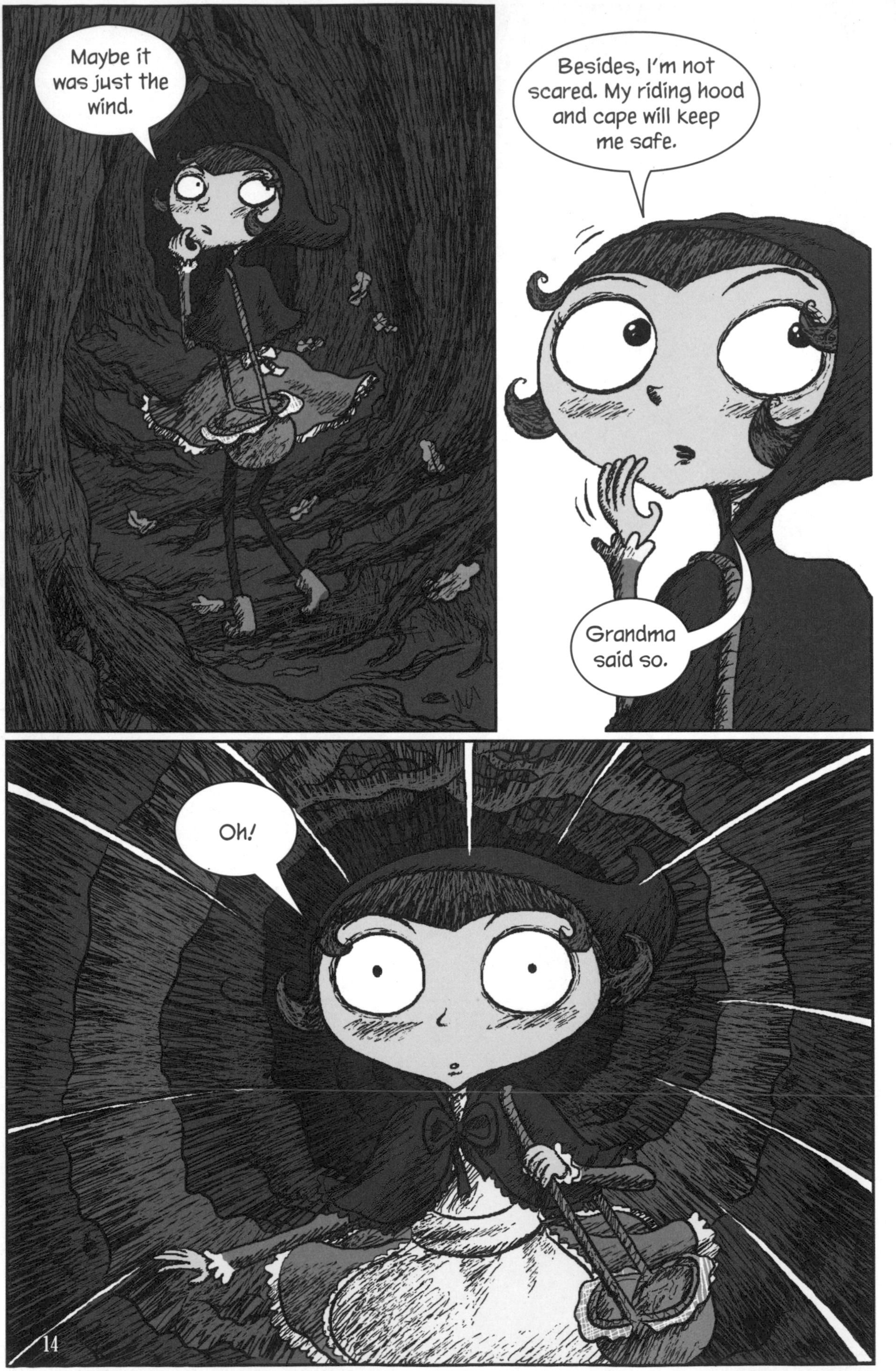
Maybe it was just the wind.
Besides, I'm not scared. My riding hood and cape will keep me safe.
Grandma said so.
Oh!

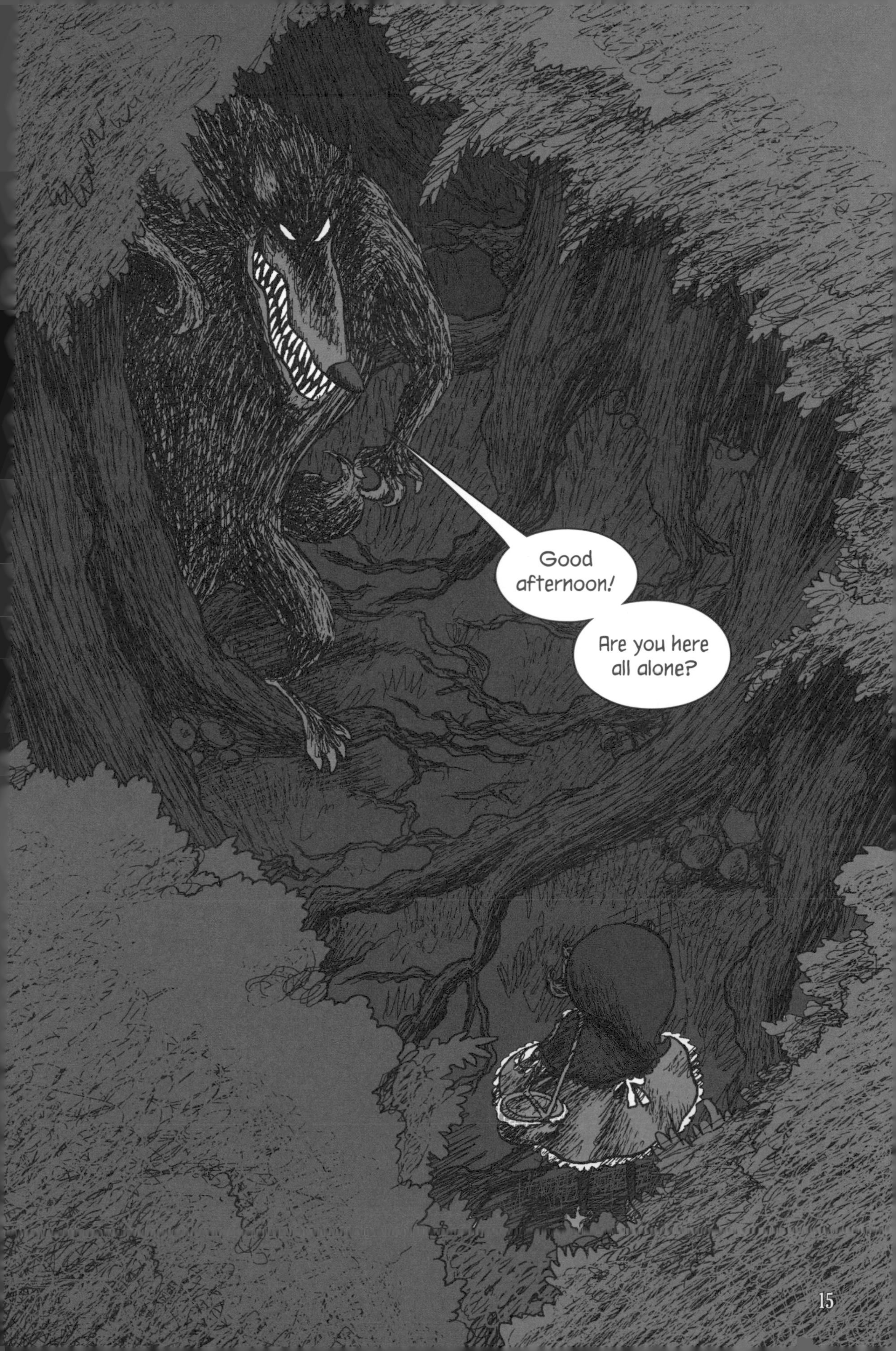
Good afternoon!
Are you here all alone?

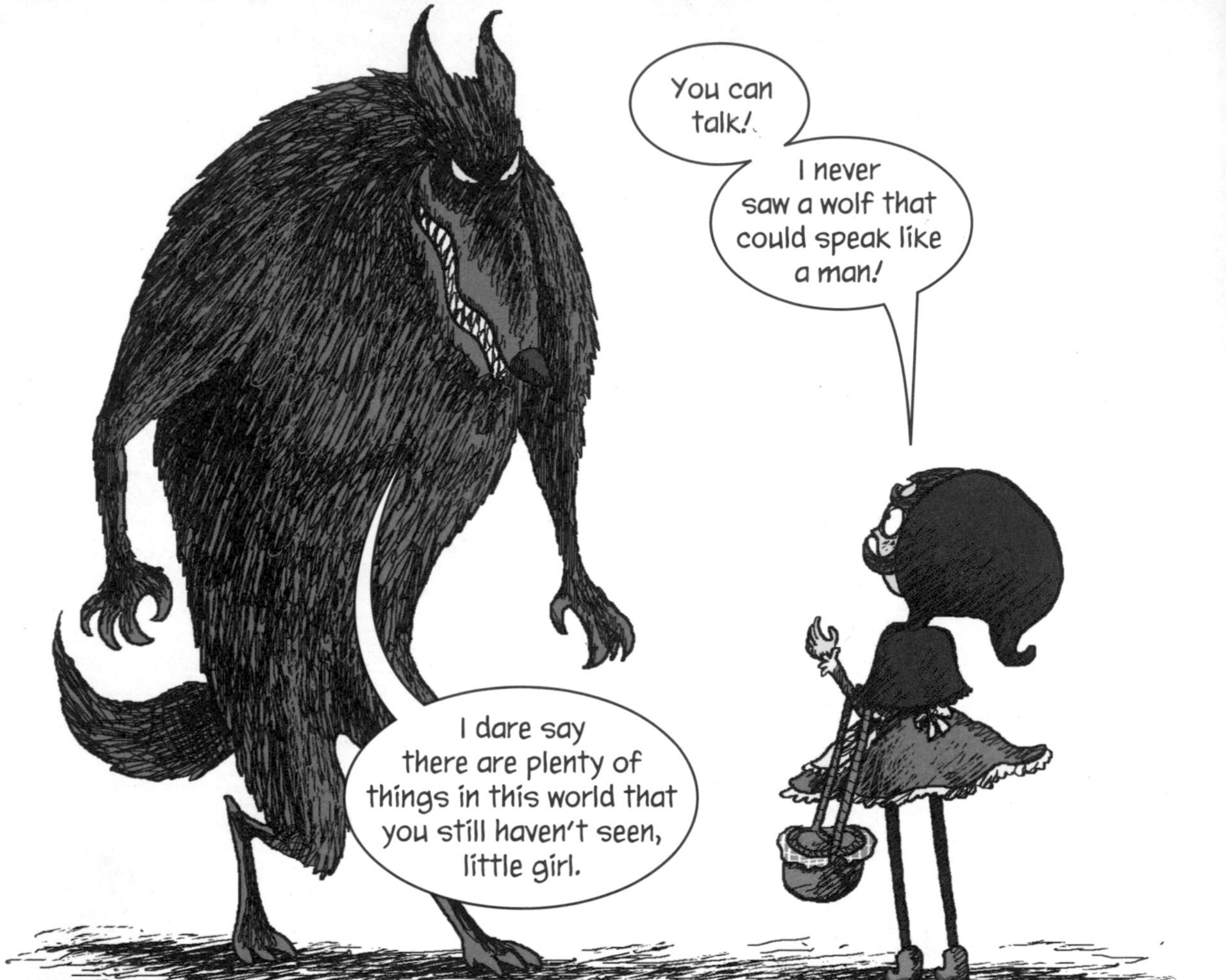
You can talk!
I never saw a wolf that could speak like a man!
I dare say there are plenty of things in this world that you still haven't seen, little girl.

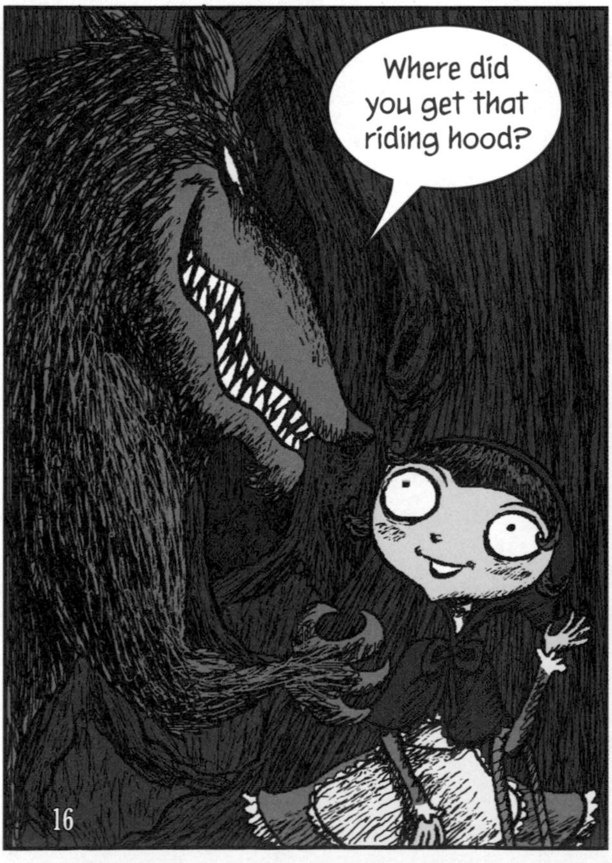
Where did you get that riding hood?

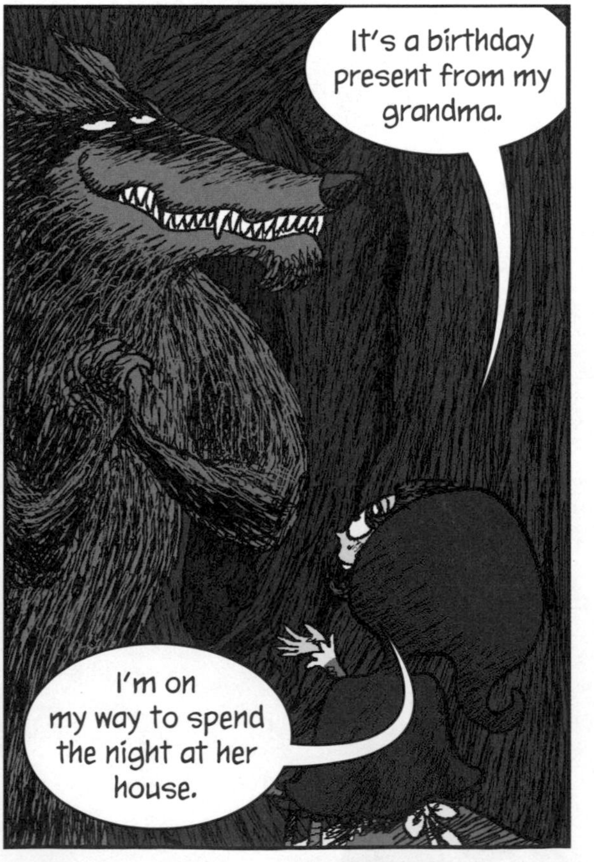
It's a birthday present from my grandma.
I'm on my way to spend the night at her house.

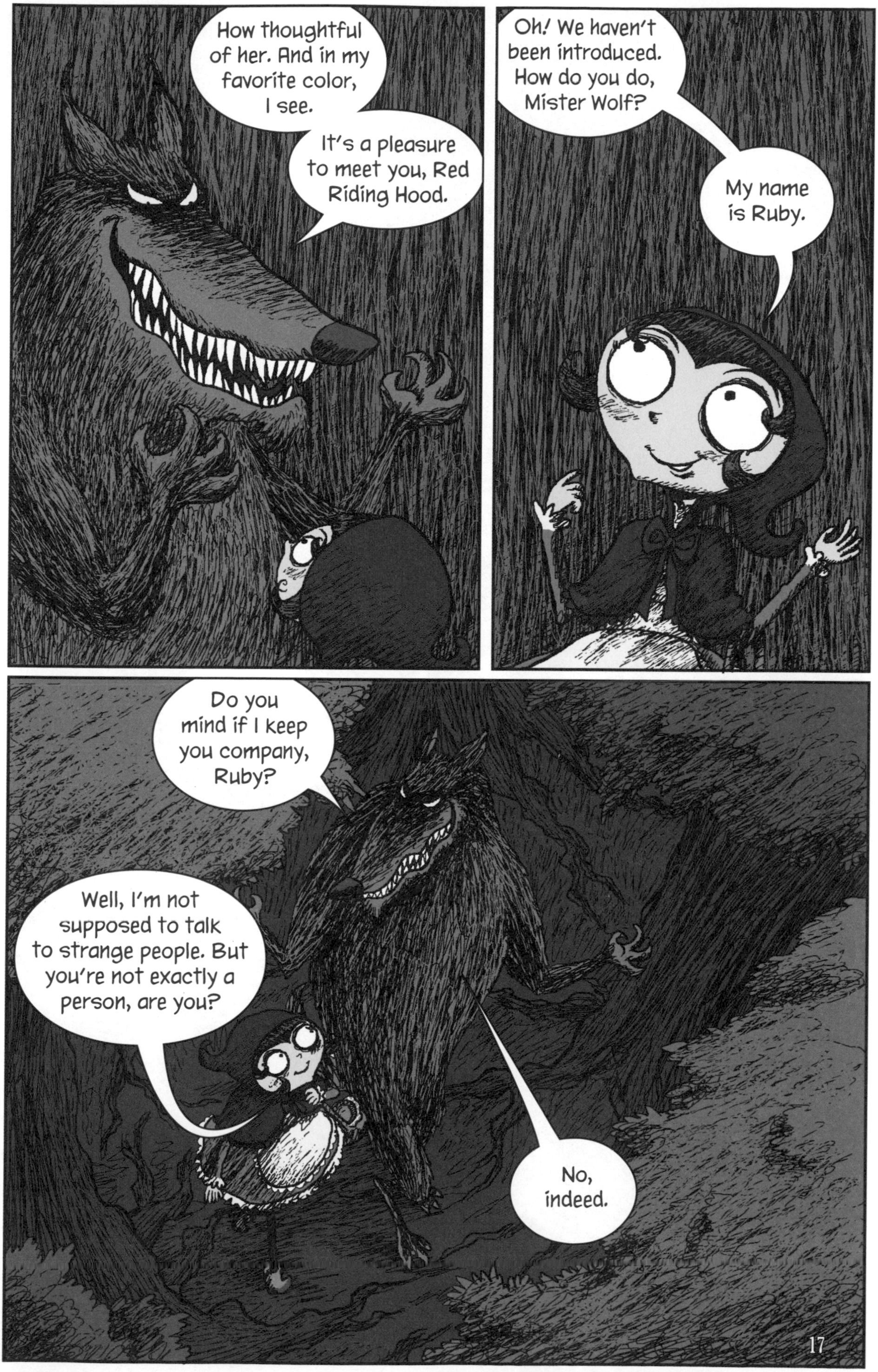
How thoughtful of her. And in my favorite color, I see.
It's a pleasure to meet you, Red Riding Hood.
Oh! We haven't been introduced. How do you do, Mister Wolf?
My name is Ruby.
Do you mind if I keep you company, Ruby?
Well, I'm not supposed to talk to strange people. But you're not exactly a person, are you?
No, indeed.

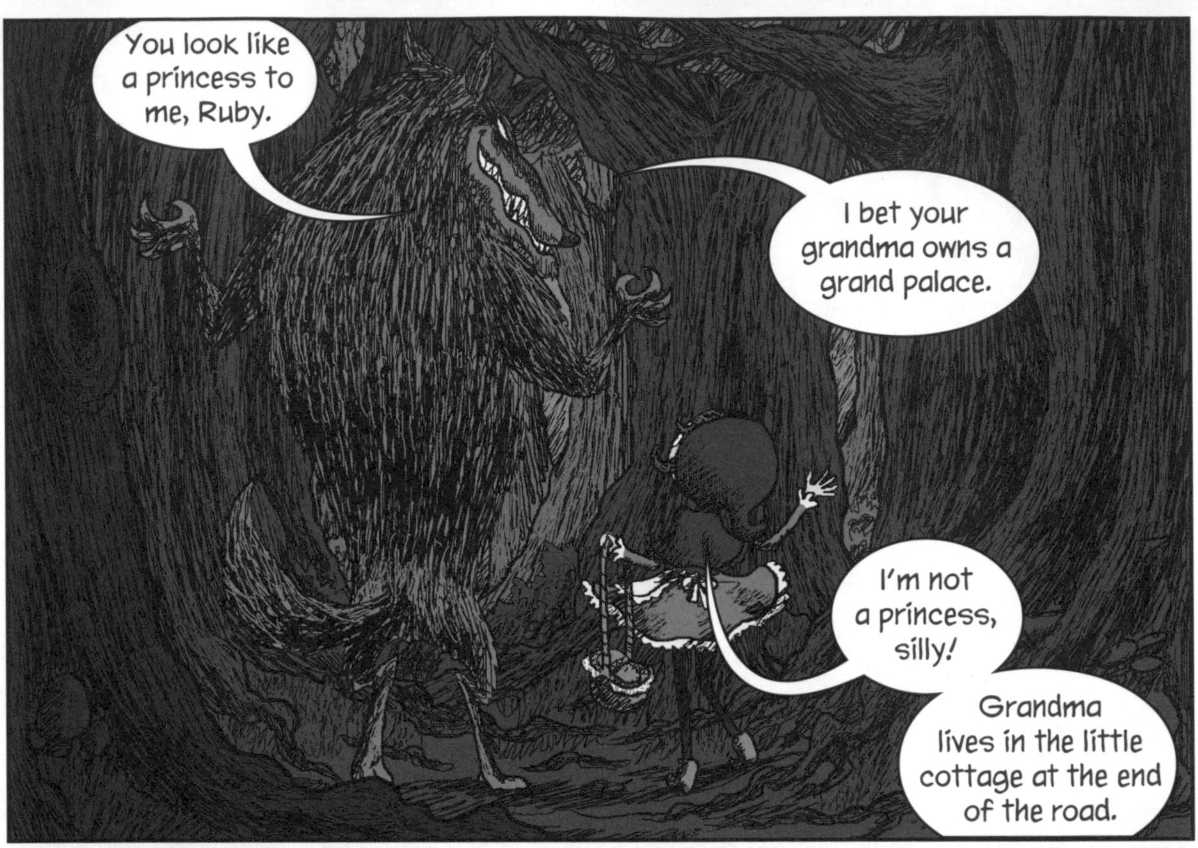
You look like a princess to me, Ruby.
I bet your grandma owns a grand palace.
I'm not a princess, silly!
Grandma lives in the little cottage at the end of the road.

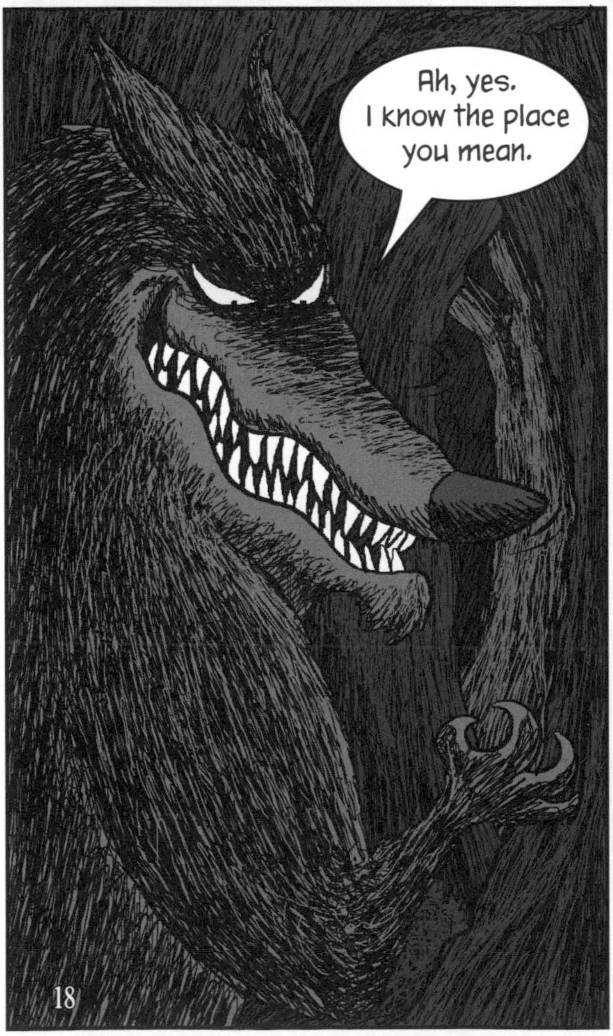
Ah, yes. I know the place you mean.

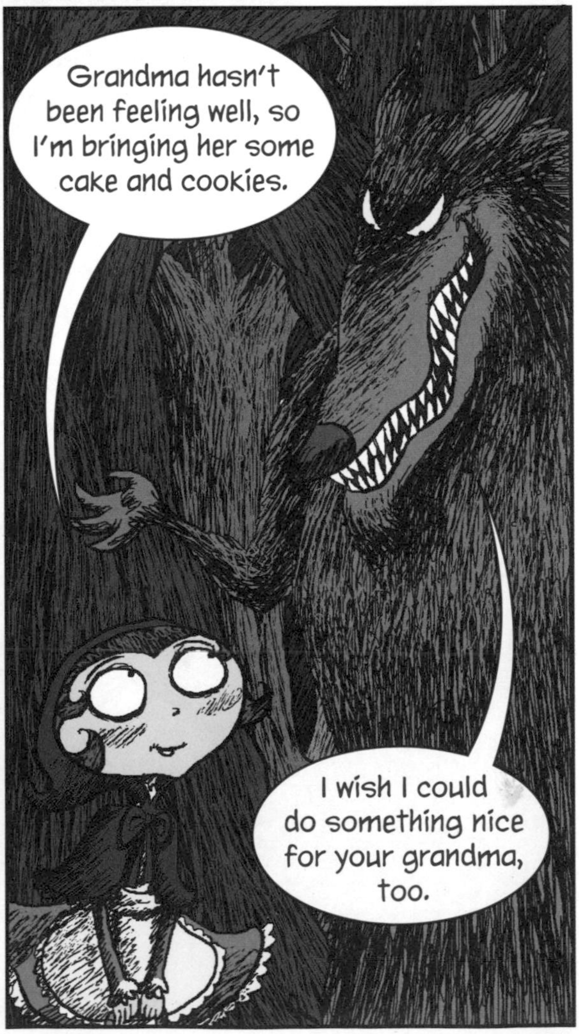
Grandma hasn't been feeling well, so I'm bringing her some cake and cookies.
I wish I could do something nice for your grandma, too.

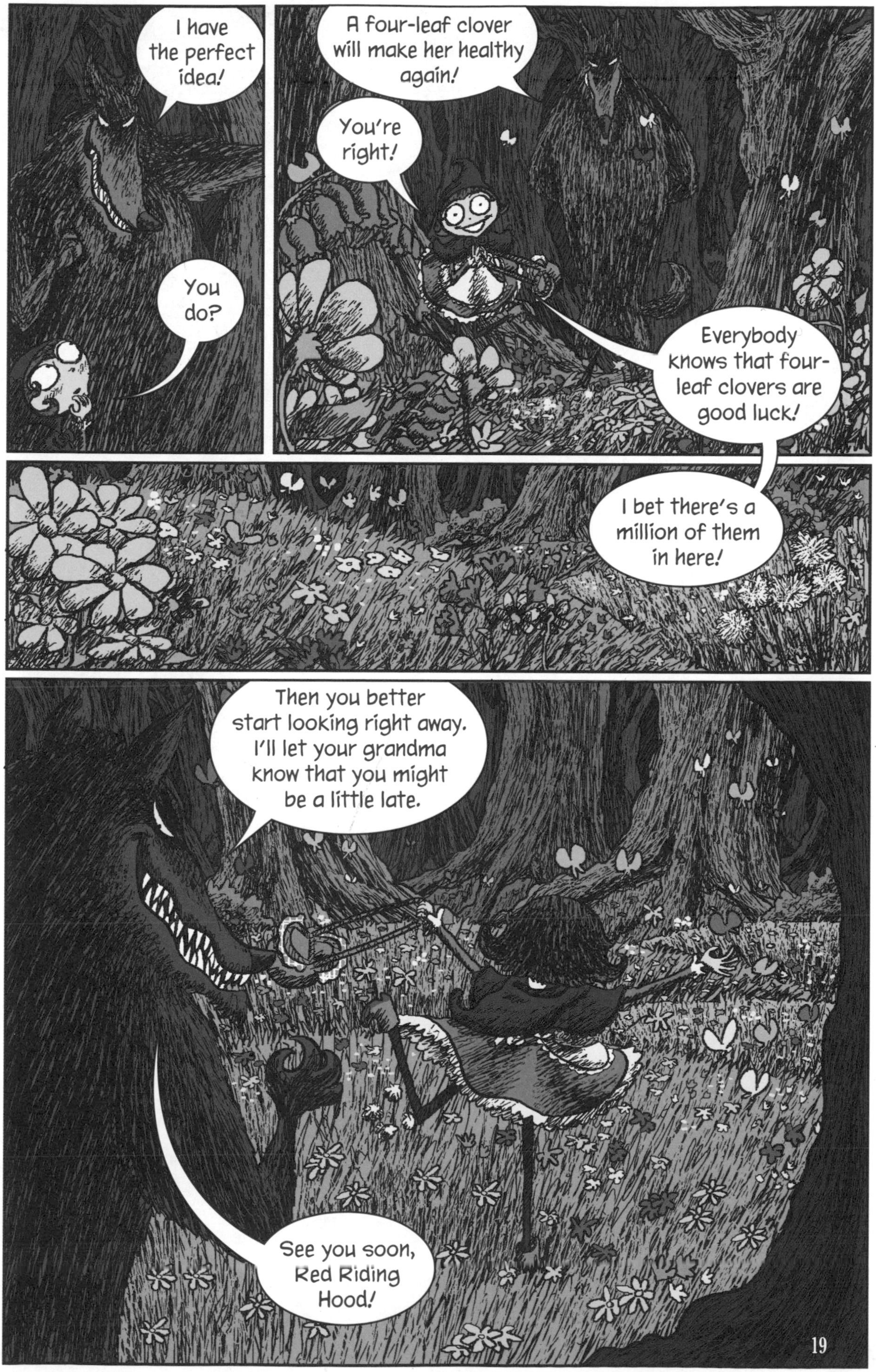

I have the perfect idea!
You do?
A four-leaf clover will make her healthy again!
You're right!
Everybody knows that four-leaf clovers are good luck!
I bet there's a million of them in here!
Then you better start looking right away. I'll let your grandma know that you might be a little late.
See you soon, Red Riding Hood!

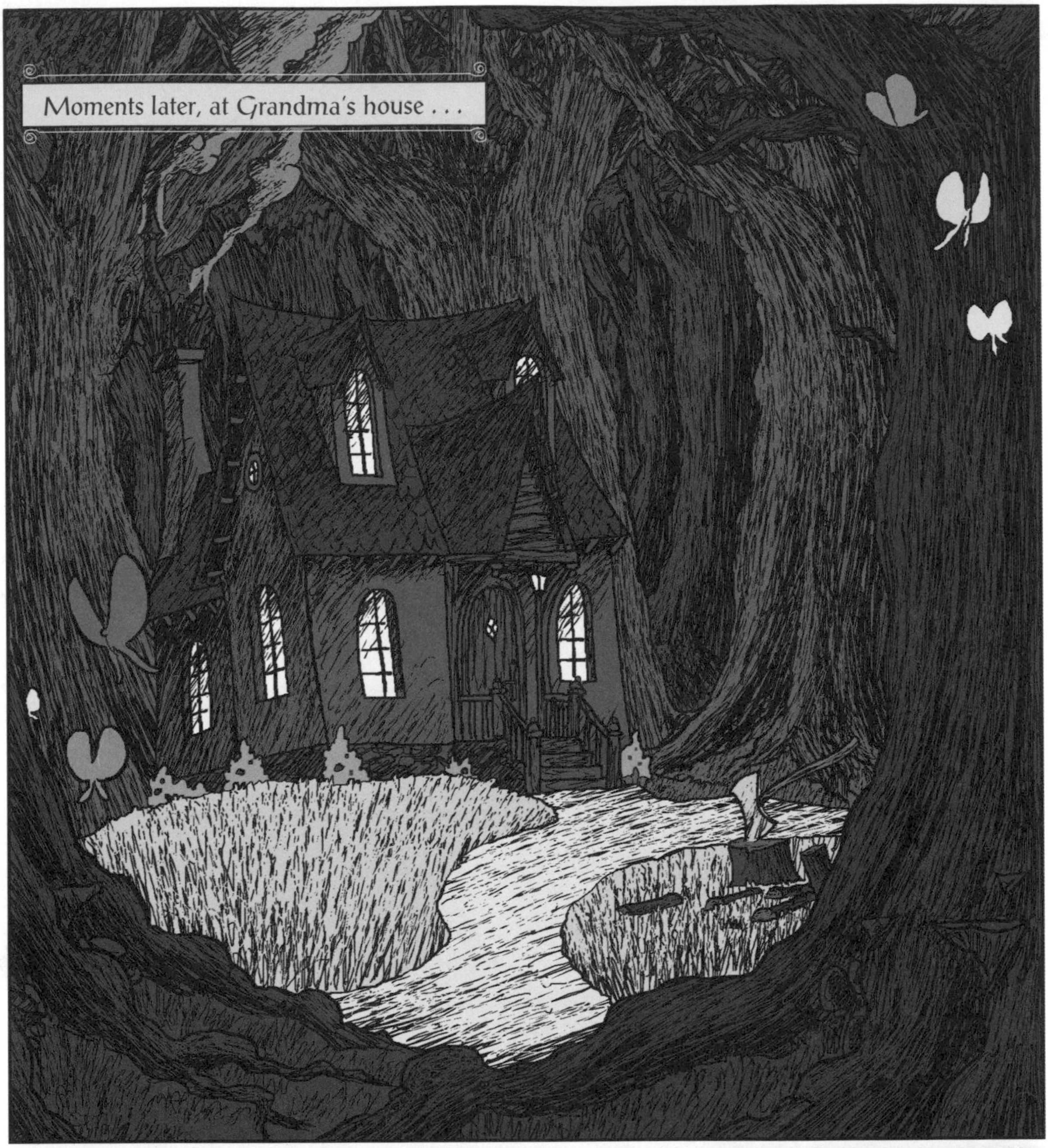
Moments later, at Grandma's house . . .

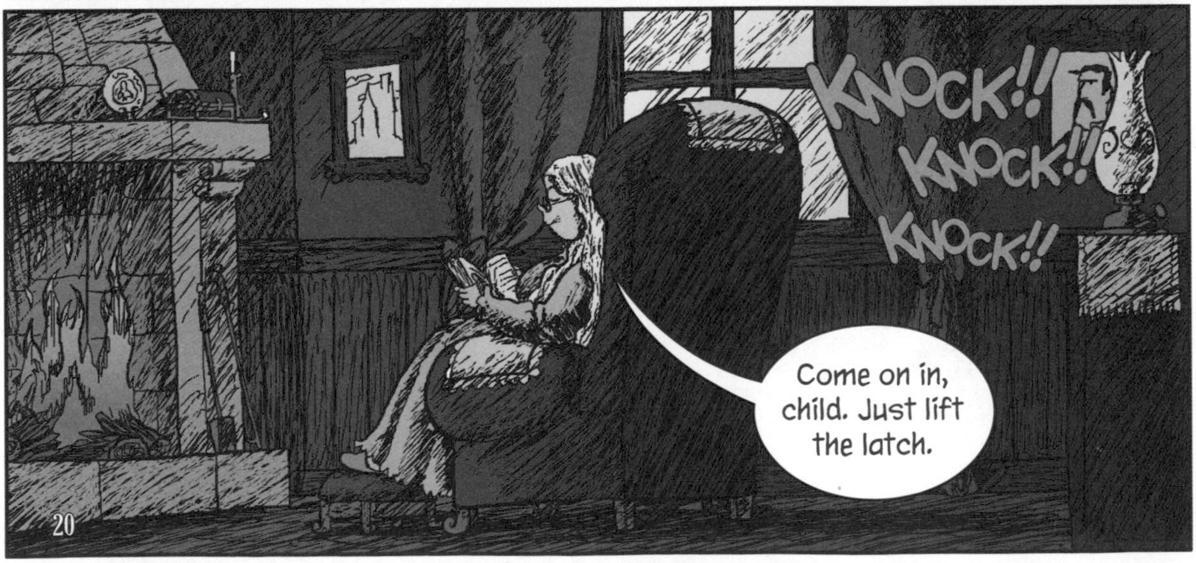
KNOCK!! KNOCK!! KNOCK!!
Come on in, child. Just lift the latch.

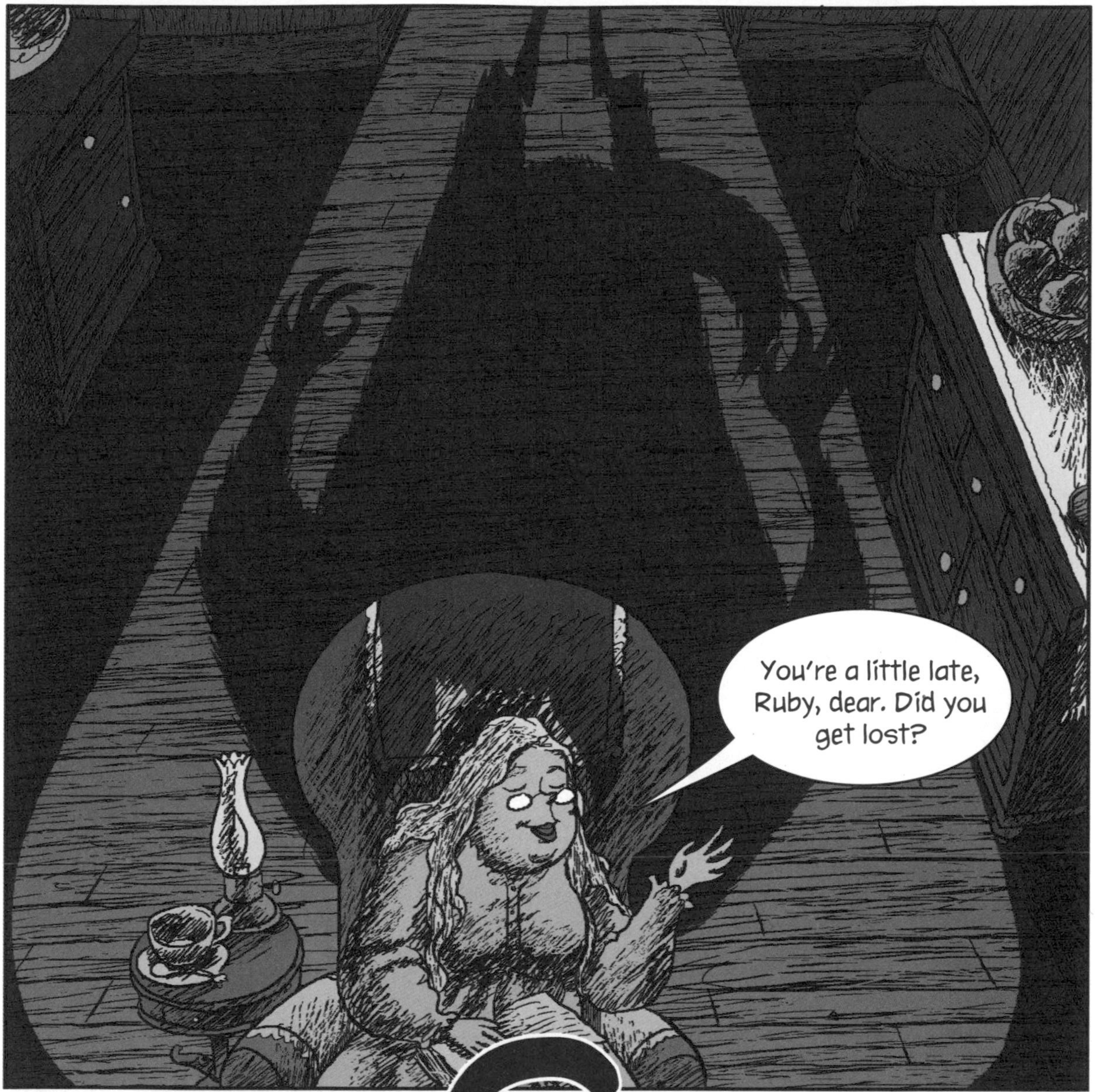
You're a little late, Ruby, dear. Did you get lost?

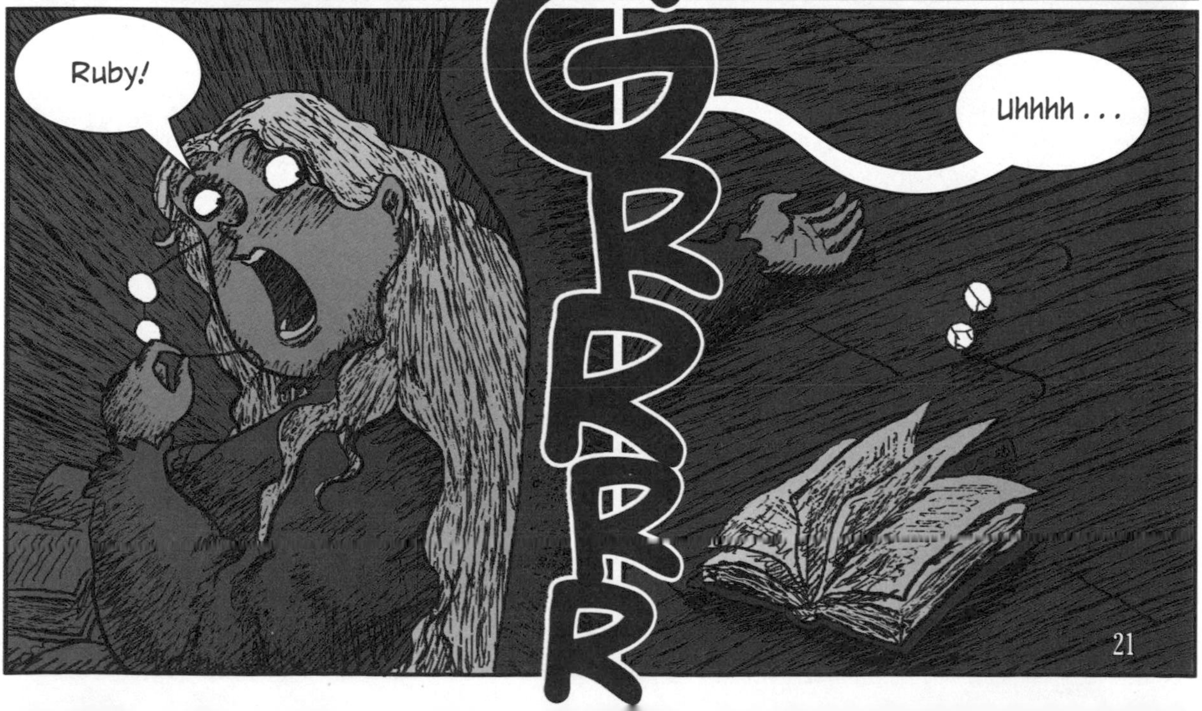
Ruby!
GRRRRRR
Uhhhh . . .

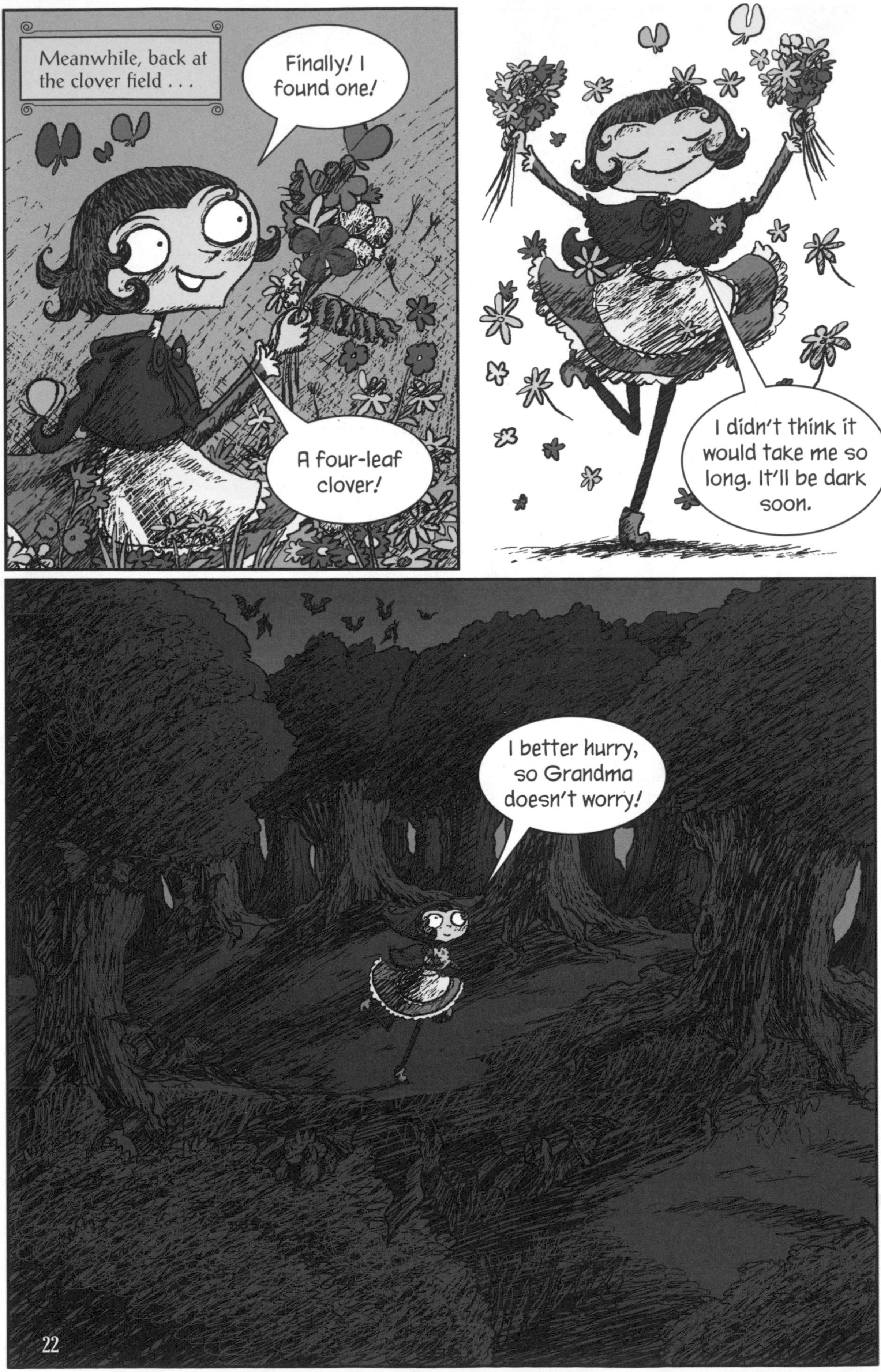

Meanwhile, back at the clover field . . .
Finally! I found one!
A four-leaf clover!
I didn't think it would take me so long. It'll be dark soon.
I better hurry, so Grandma doesn't worry!

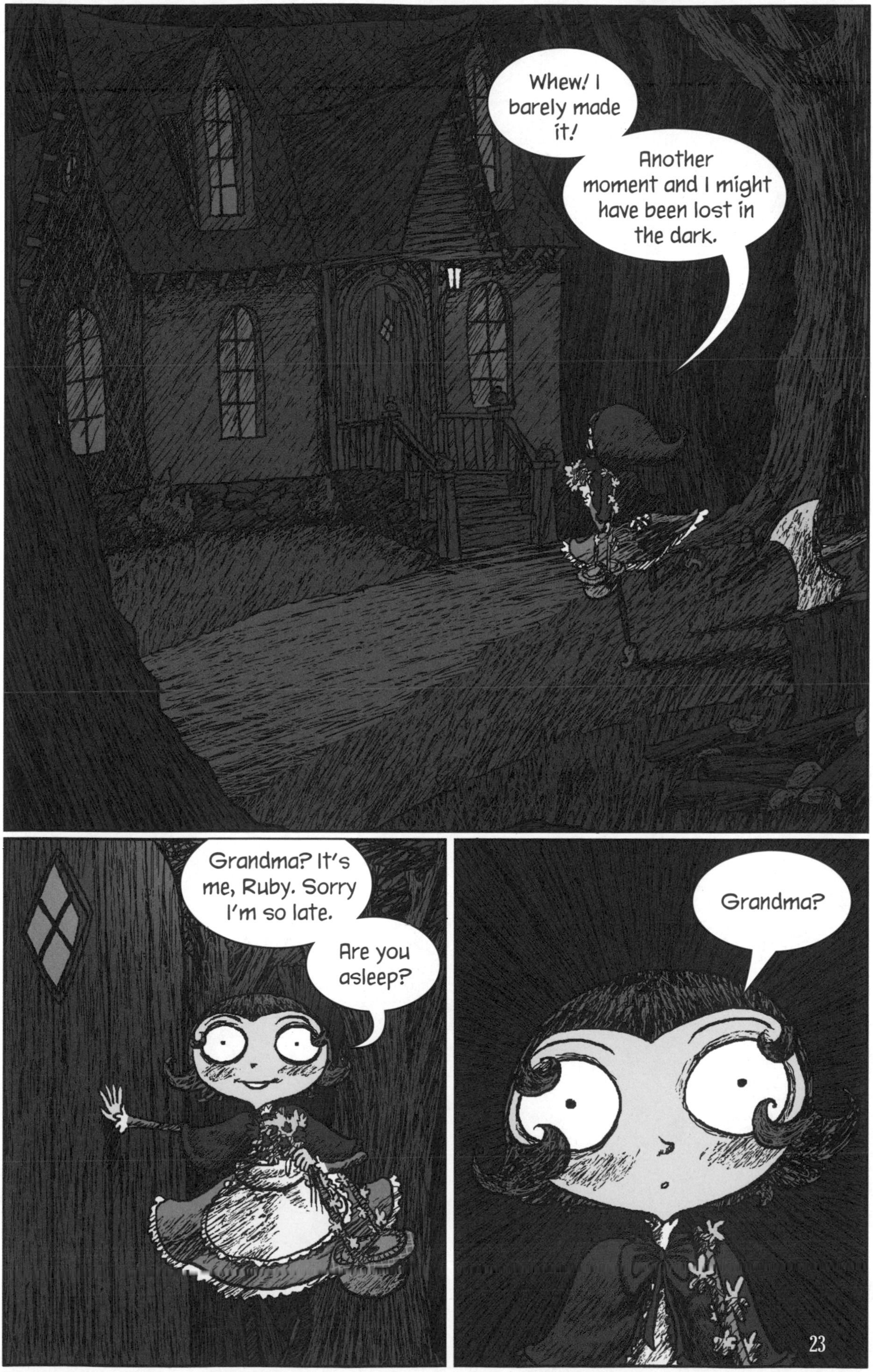
Whew! I barely made it!
Another moment and I might have been lost in the dark.
Grandma? It's me, Ruby. Sorry I'm so late.
Are you asleep?
Grandma?

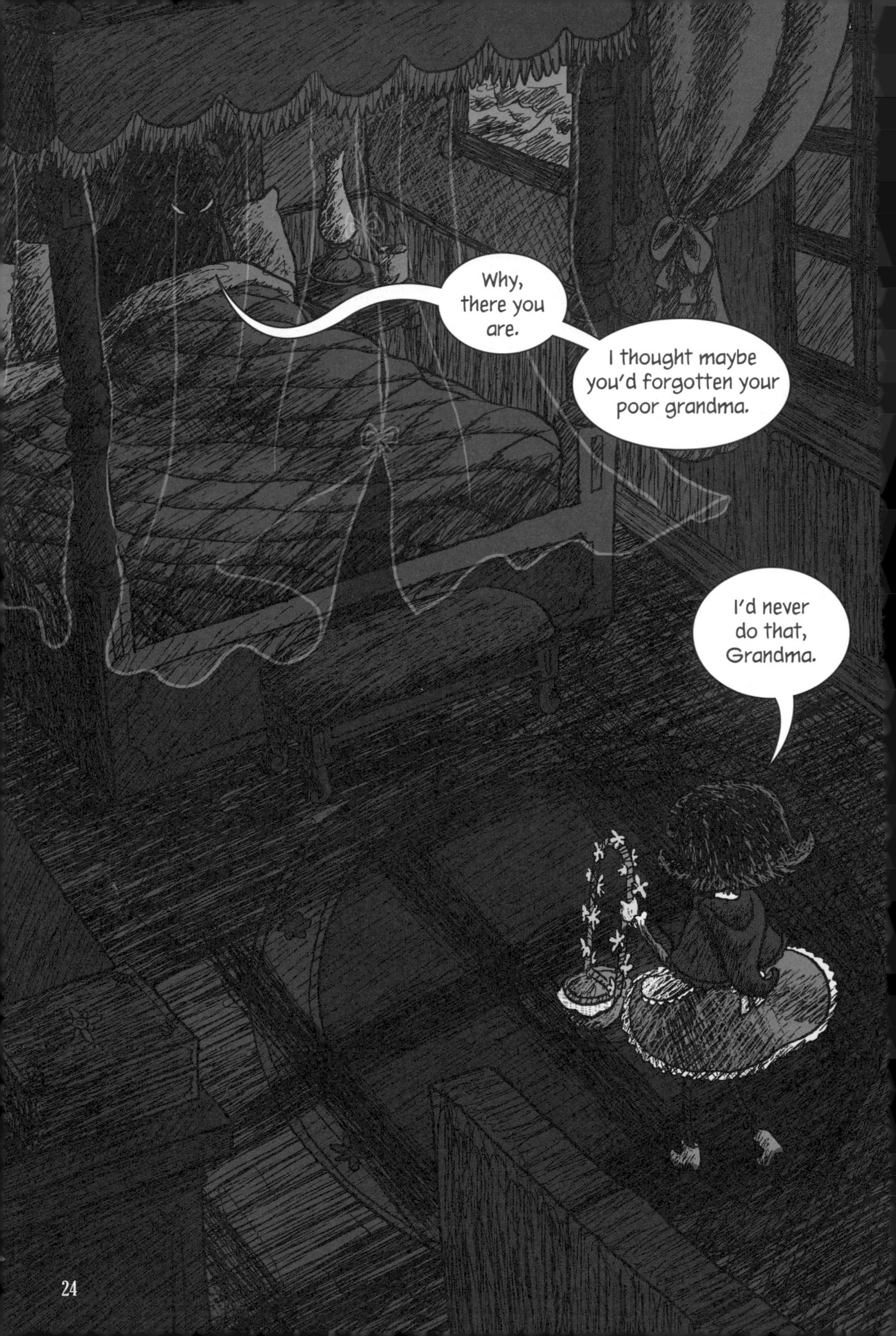
Why, there you are.
I thought maybe you'd forgotten your poor grandma.
I'd never do that, Grandma.

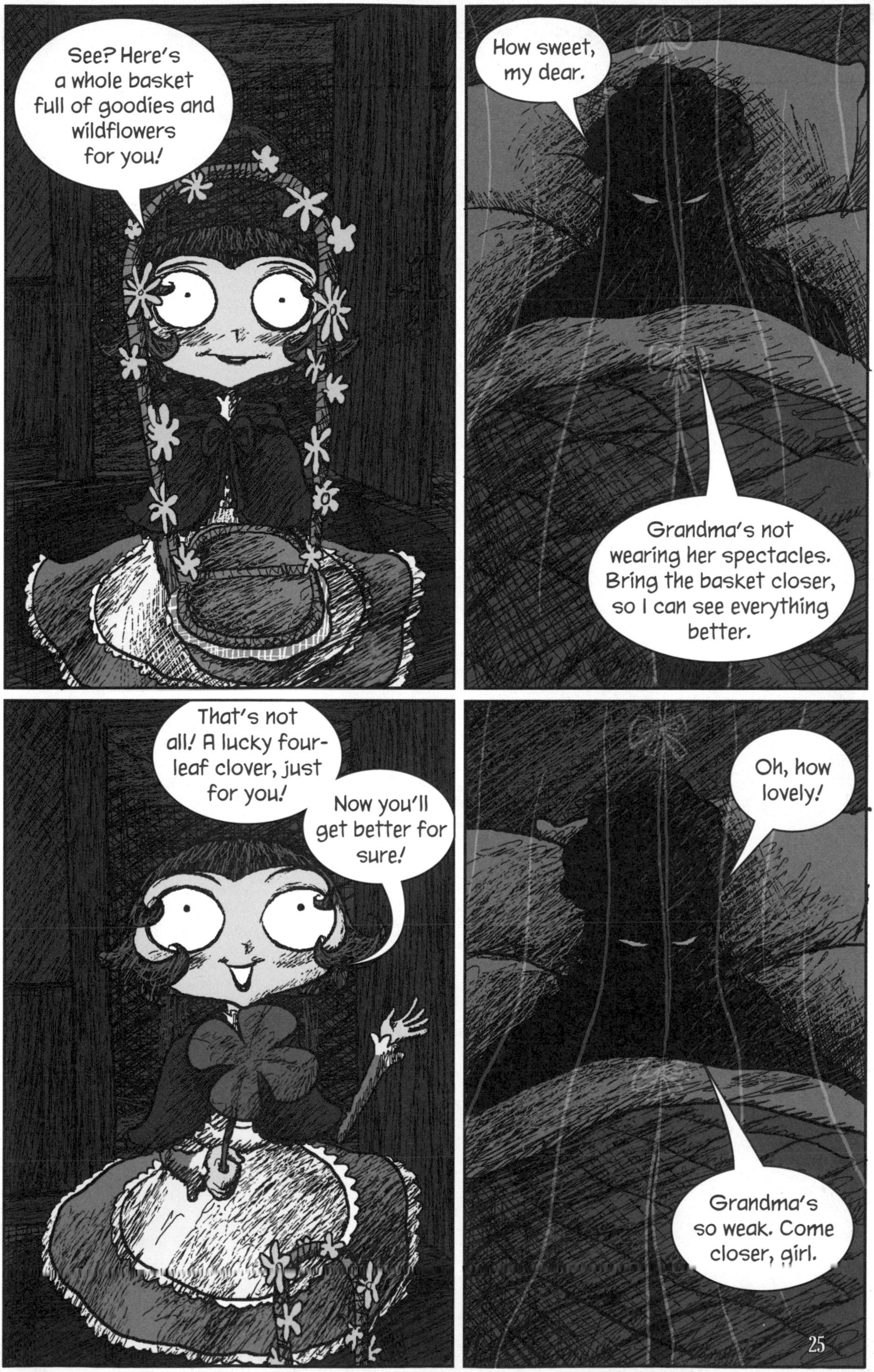
See? Here's a whole basket full of goodies and wildflowers for you!
How sweet, my dear.
Grandma's not wearing her spectacles. Bring the basket closer, so I can see everything better.
That's not all! A lucky four-leaf clover, just for you!
Now you'll get better for sure!
Oh, how lovely!
Grandma's so weak. Come closer, girl.

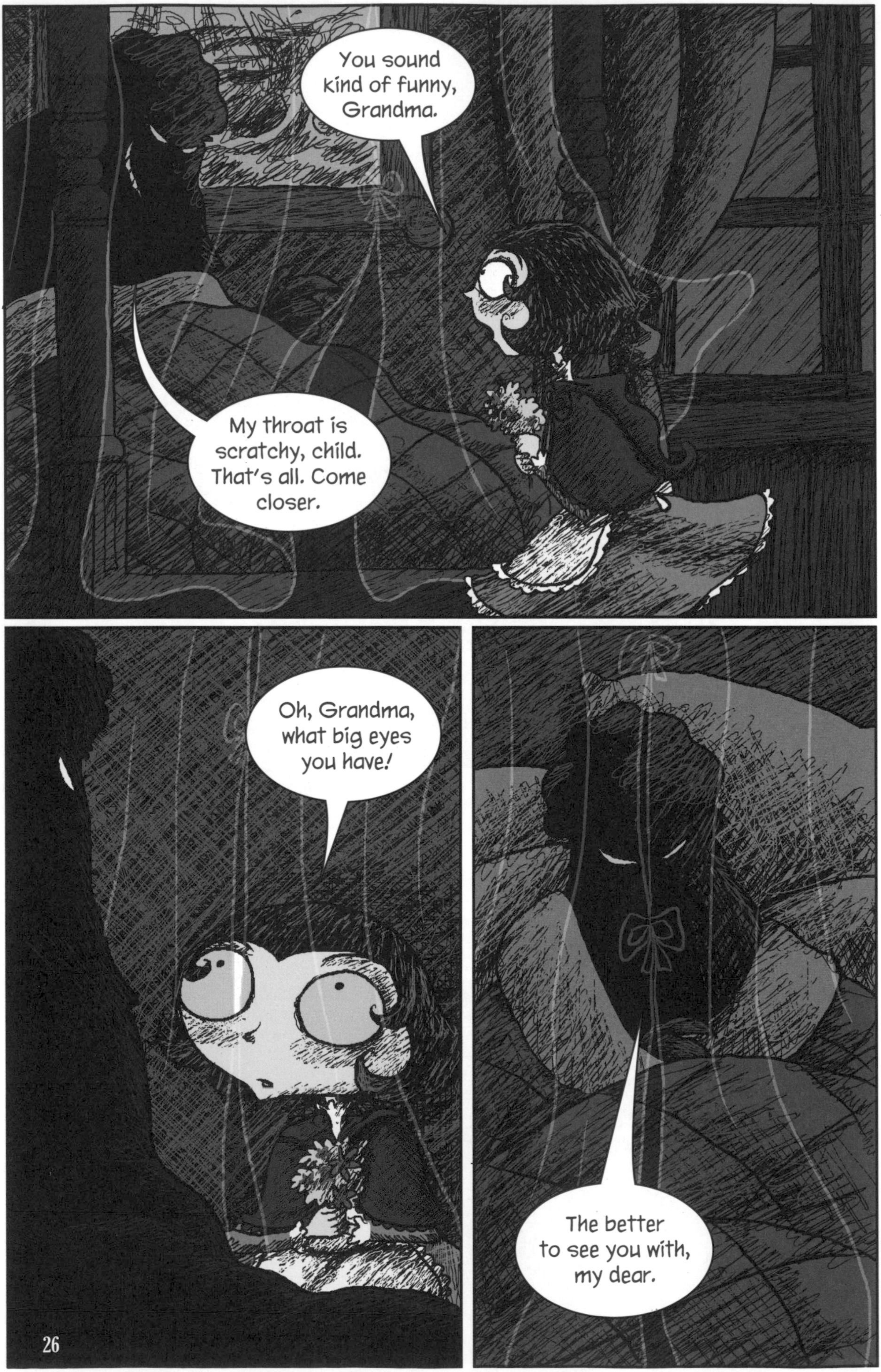
You sound kind of funny, Grandma.
My throat is scratchy, child. That's all. Come closer.
Oh, Grandma, what big eyes you have!
The better to see you with, my dear.

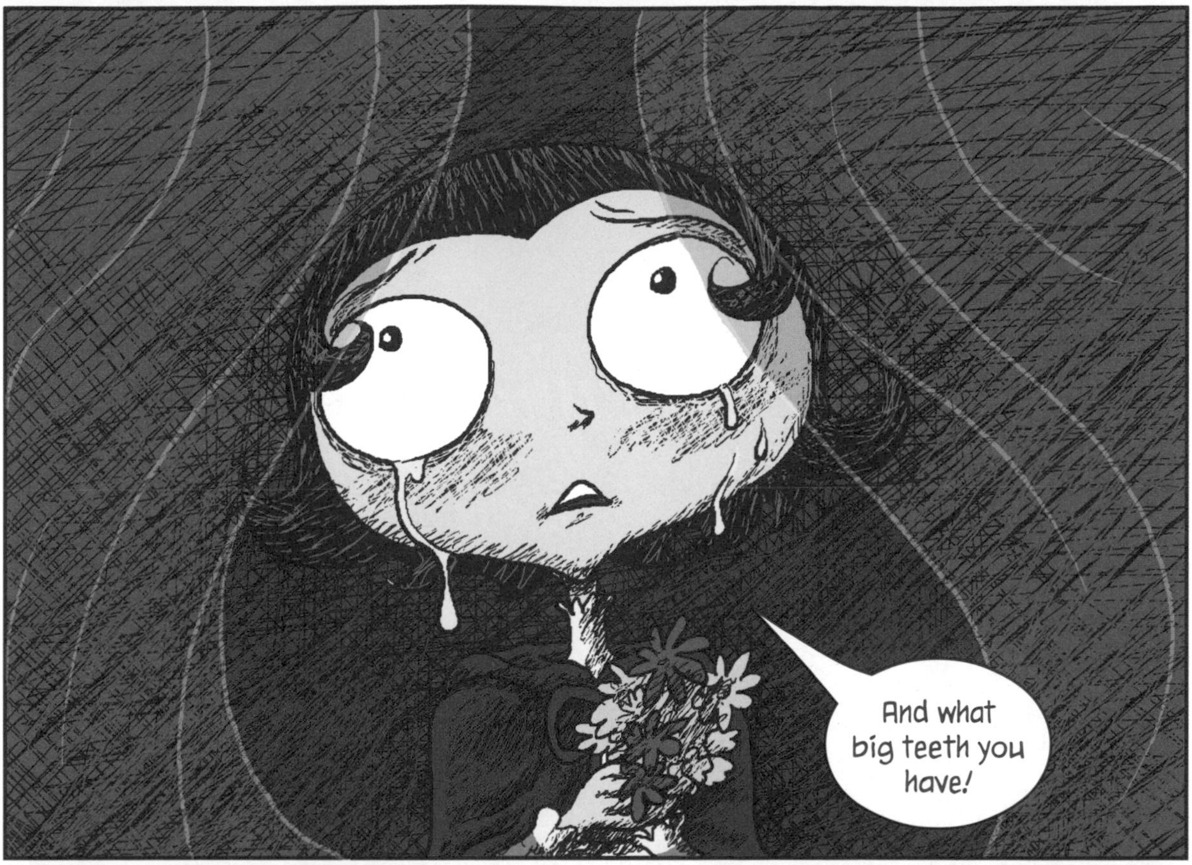
And what big teeth you have!

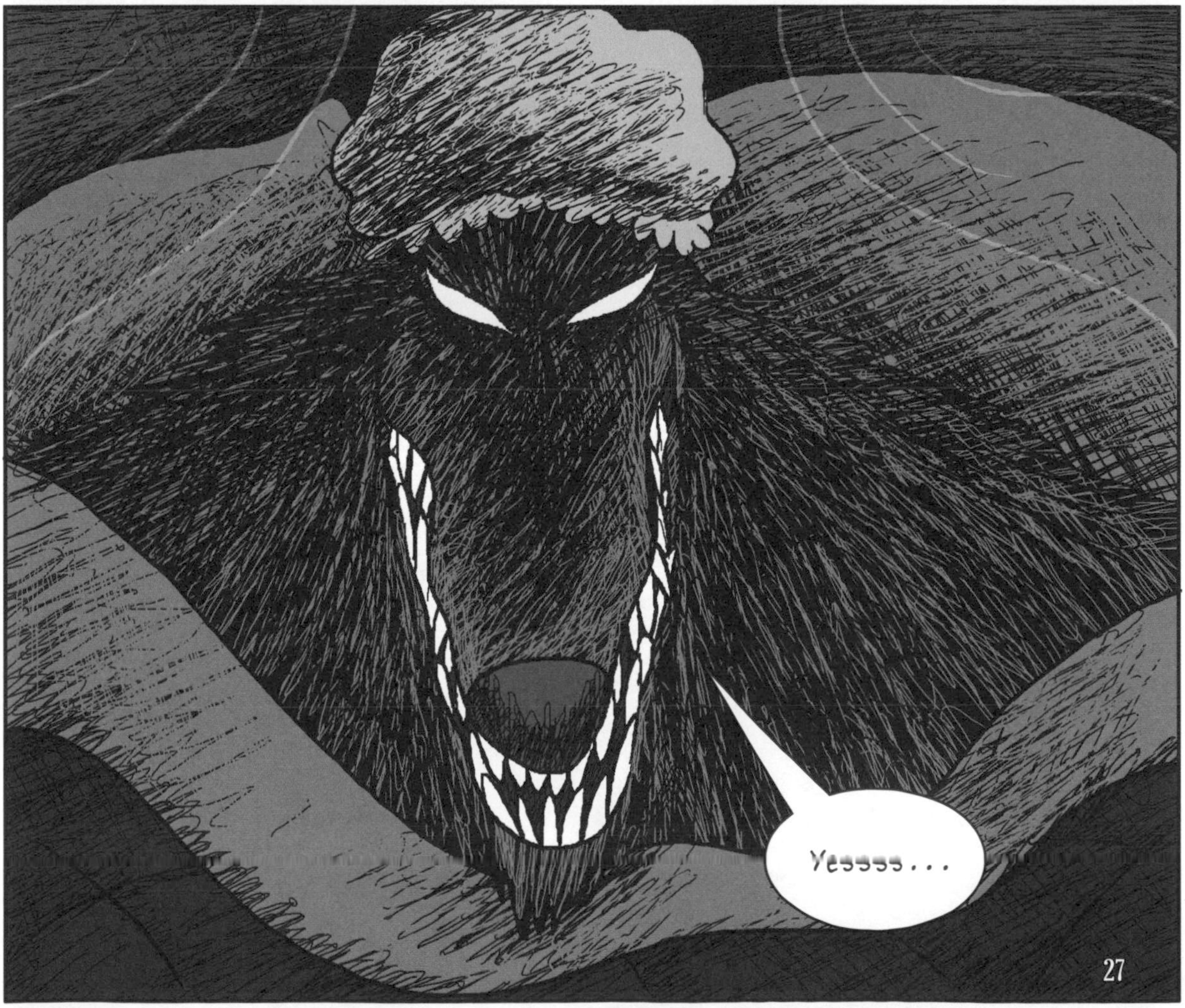
Yessss . . .

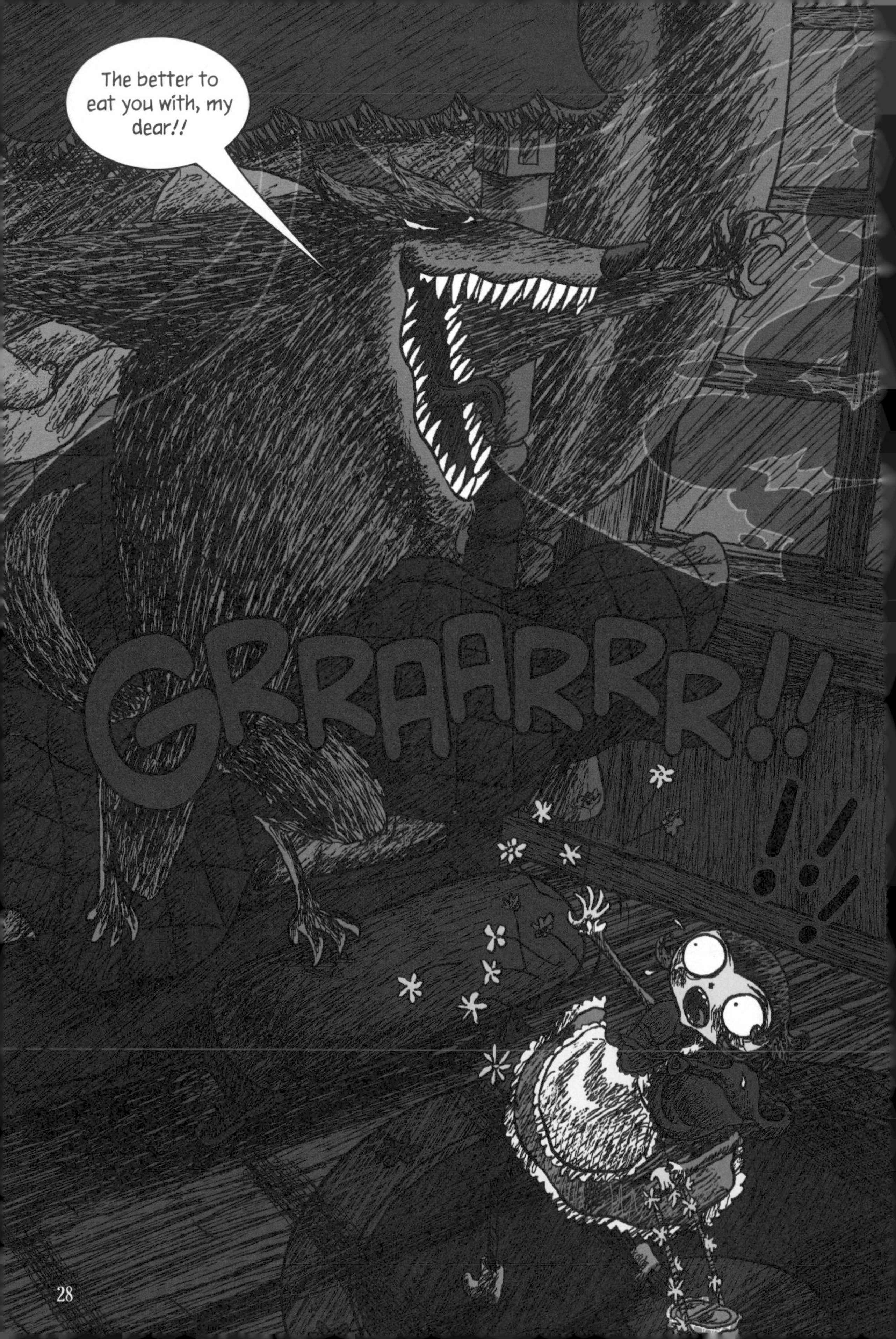
The better to eat you with, my dear!!
GRRAARRR!!
!!

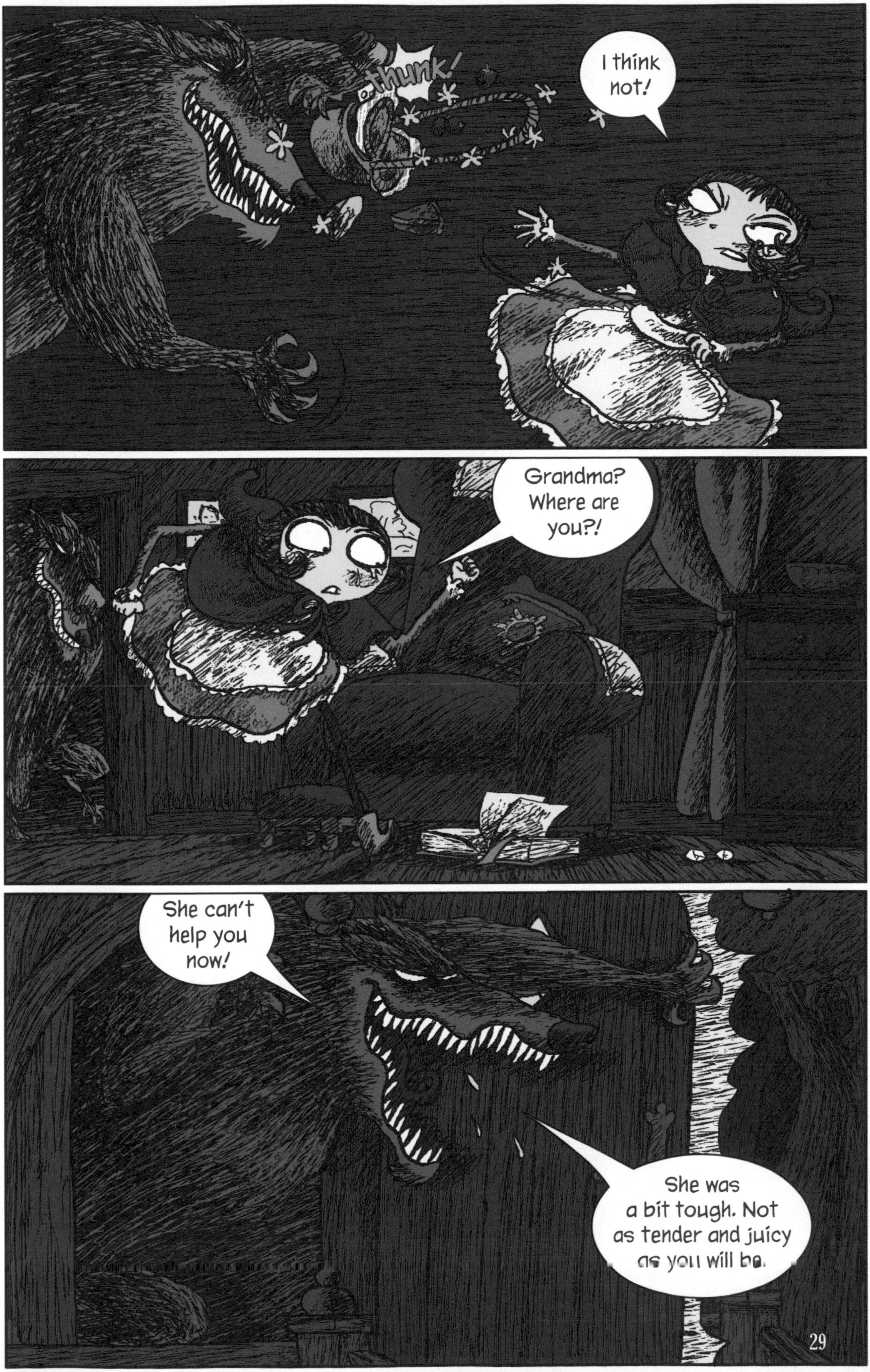
thunk!
I think not!
Grandma? Where are you?!
She can't help you now!
She was a bit tough. Not as tender and juicy as you will be.

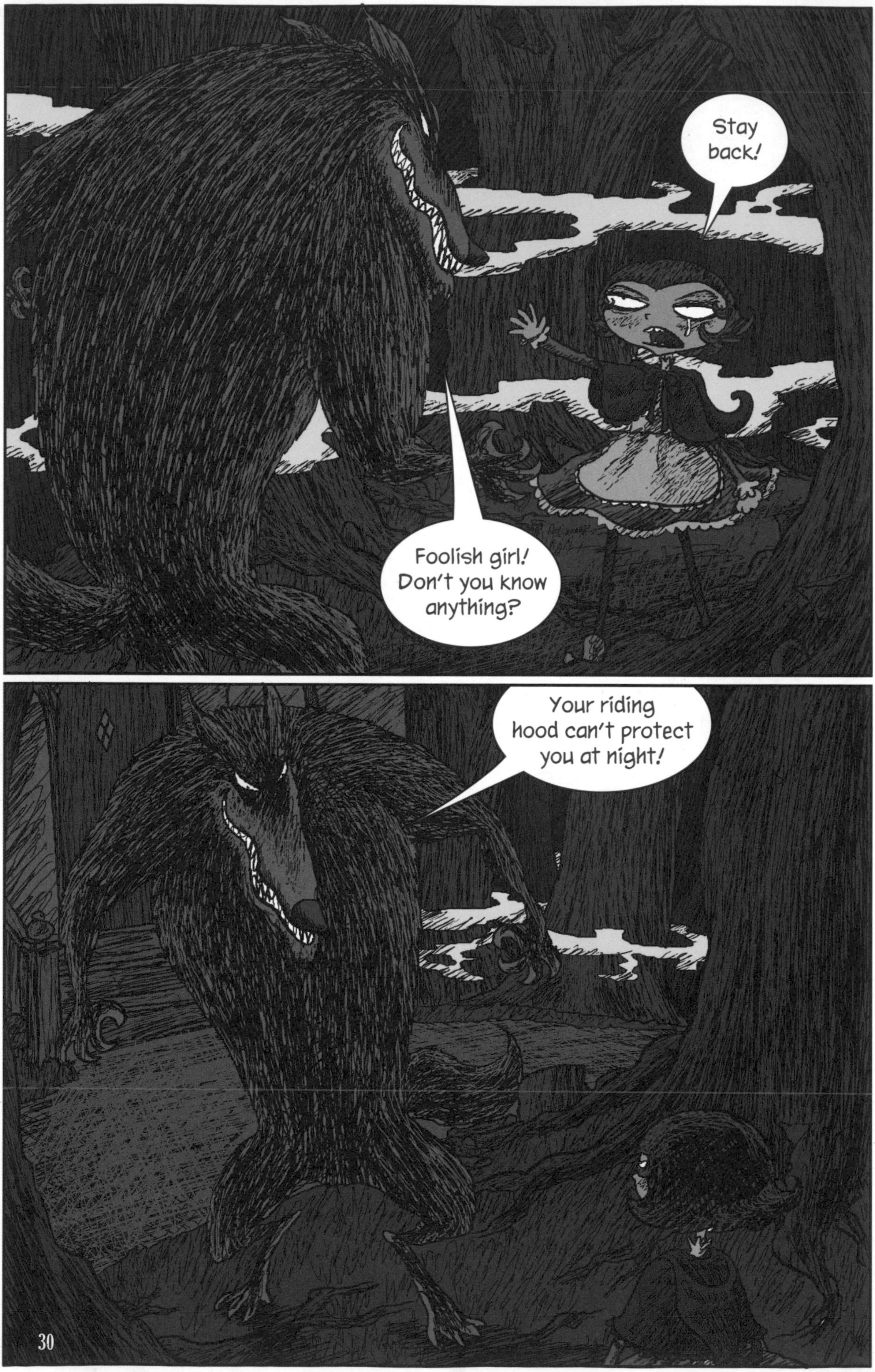
Stay back!
Foolish girl! Don't you know anything?
Your riding hood can't protect you at night!

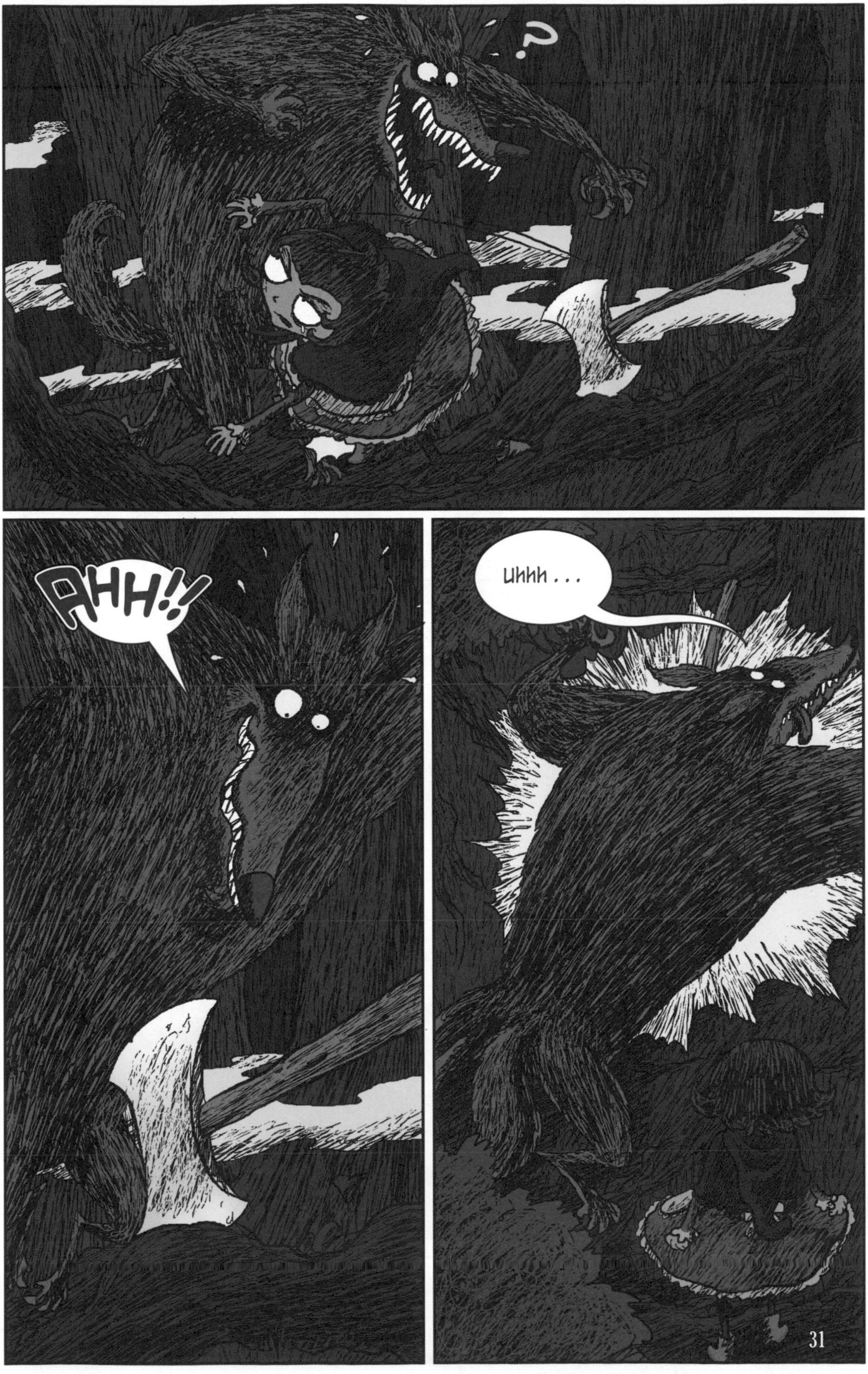
?
AHH!!
uhhh . . .

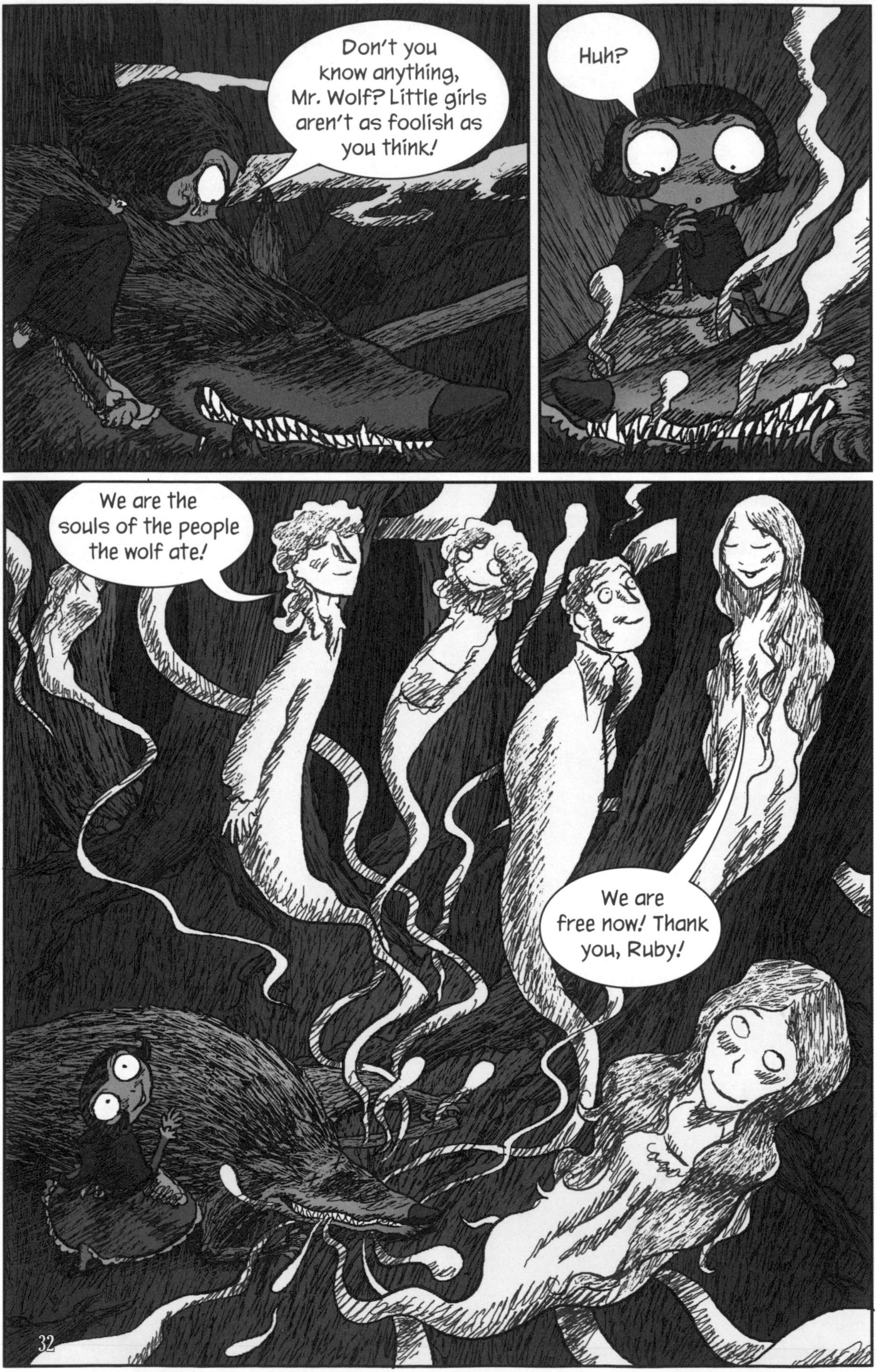
Don't you know anything, Mr. Wolf? Little girls aren't as foolish as you think!
Huh?
We are the souls of the people the wolf ate!
We are free now! Thank you, Ruby!

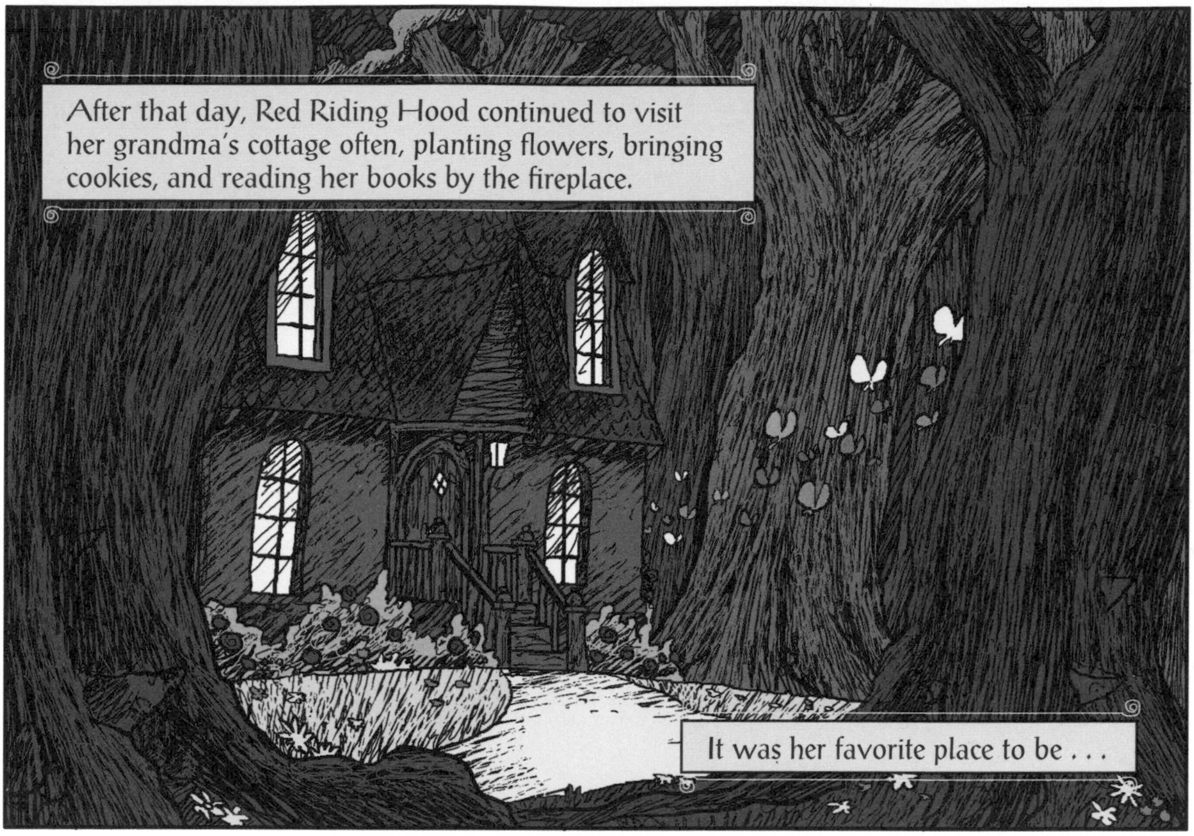
After that day, Red Riding Hood continued to visit her grandma's cottage often, planting flowers, bringing cookies, and reading her books by the fireplace.
It was her favorite place to be . . .

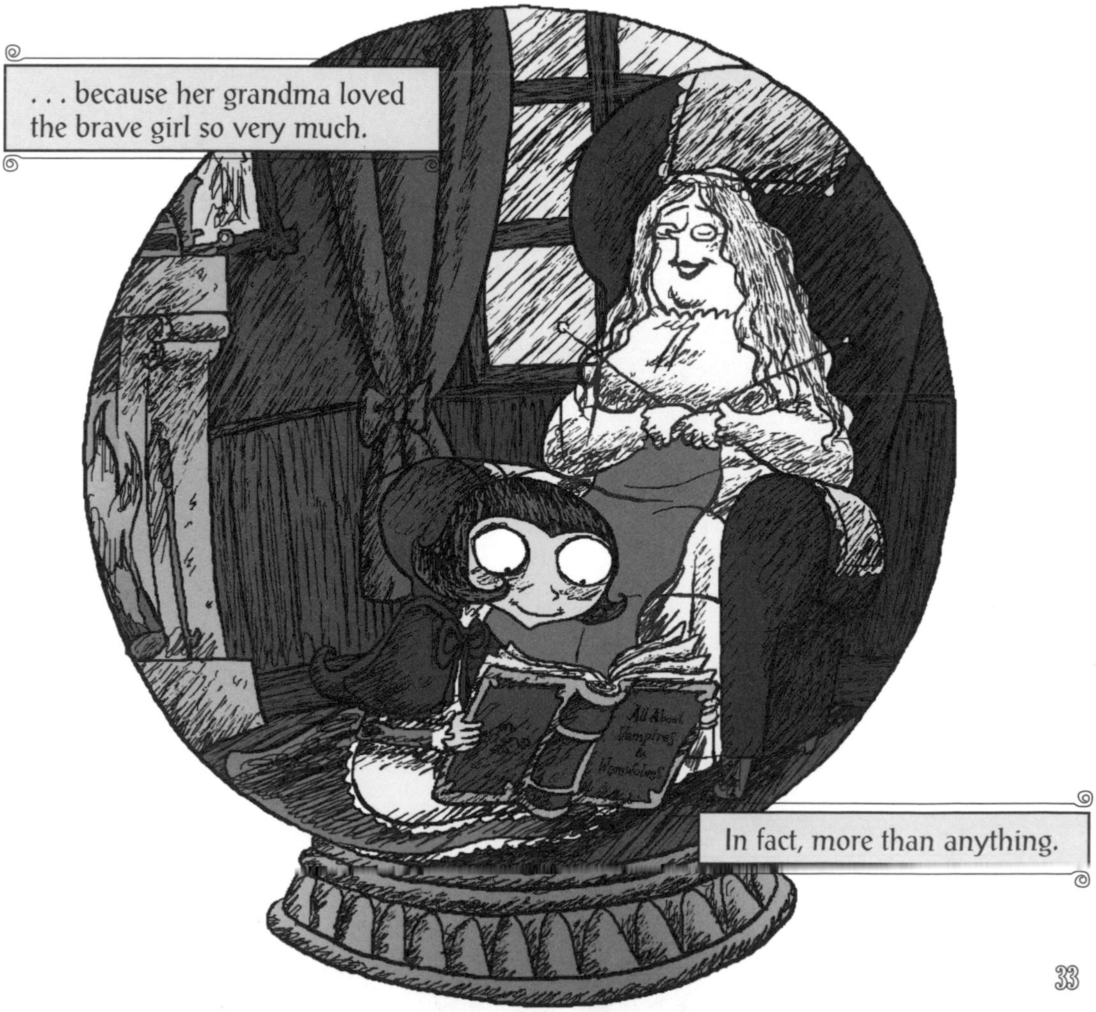
. . . because her grandma loved the brave girl so very much.
In fact, more than anything.

# About the Author

Since 1986, Martin Powell has been a freelance writer. He has written hundreds of stories, many of which have been published by Disney, Marvel, Tekno Comix, Moonstone Books, and others. In 1989, Powell received an Eisner Award nomination for his graphic novel *Scarlet in Gaslight.* This award is one of the highest comic book honors.

# About the Illustrator

Victor Rivas was born and raised in Vigo, Spain, and he now lives outside of Barcelona. Rivas has been a freelance illustrator since 1987, working on children and teen books, as well as magazines, posters, game animation, and comics. When he's not working, Rivas enjoys reading comics, watching cartoons and films, and playing strategy games. Most importantly, he spends as much time as possible with his daughter, Marta.

# Glossary

**cottage** (KOT-ij)—a small house

**crystal ball** (KRISS-tul BAWL)—a clear ball made of crystal that is used to see the future

**foolish** (FOOL-ish)—slow, stupid, or unwise

**latch** (LACH)—a lock or handle for a door

**palace** (PAL-iss)—a large, grand home for a ruler or wealthy person

**riding hood** (RYDE-ing HUD)—a cloak with a hood attached that a woman wears while riding a horse

**souls** (SOLZ)—the spiritual parts of people

**spectacles** (SPEK-tuh-kuhlz)—eyeglasses

**tender** (TEN-dur)—soft

**wildflowers** (WILDE-flou-urz)—pretty flowers that grow in the wild

**wiser** (WIZ-ur)—smarter or more experienced

# The History of
# Red Riding Hood

Many scholars believe the story of **Red Riding Hood** began as a folktale hundreds of years ago. These stories were passed down orally from generation to generation. In 1697, French author Charles Perrault wrote down the earliest known version of the story for his book *Tales of Mother Goose.* Perrault's tale, known as "Le Petit Chaperon Rouge," was different from many modern versions. In his tale, Red Riding Hood is eaten by the wolf and does not escape. Perrault knew this tragic ending would scare his readers. He wanted his story to teach a moral, or a lesson in right and wrong. In fact, at the end of the story the author left a message for his reader, stating, "Children . . . should never talk to strangers, for if they should do so, they may well provide dinner for a wolf."

Perrault's tale was popular during its time, but today's best-known version came many years later. In 1812, Jacob and Wilhelm Grimm published their book of collected stories called *Children's and Household Tales.* It included several of today's most famous fairy tales, such as "Cinderella," "Snow White," and "Rapunzel." The book also included the story of **Red Riding Hood**, which they called "Little Red Cap." Although similar to Perrault's version, "Little Red Cap" was intended to be read by children.

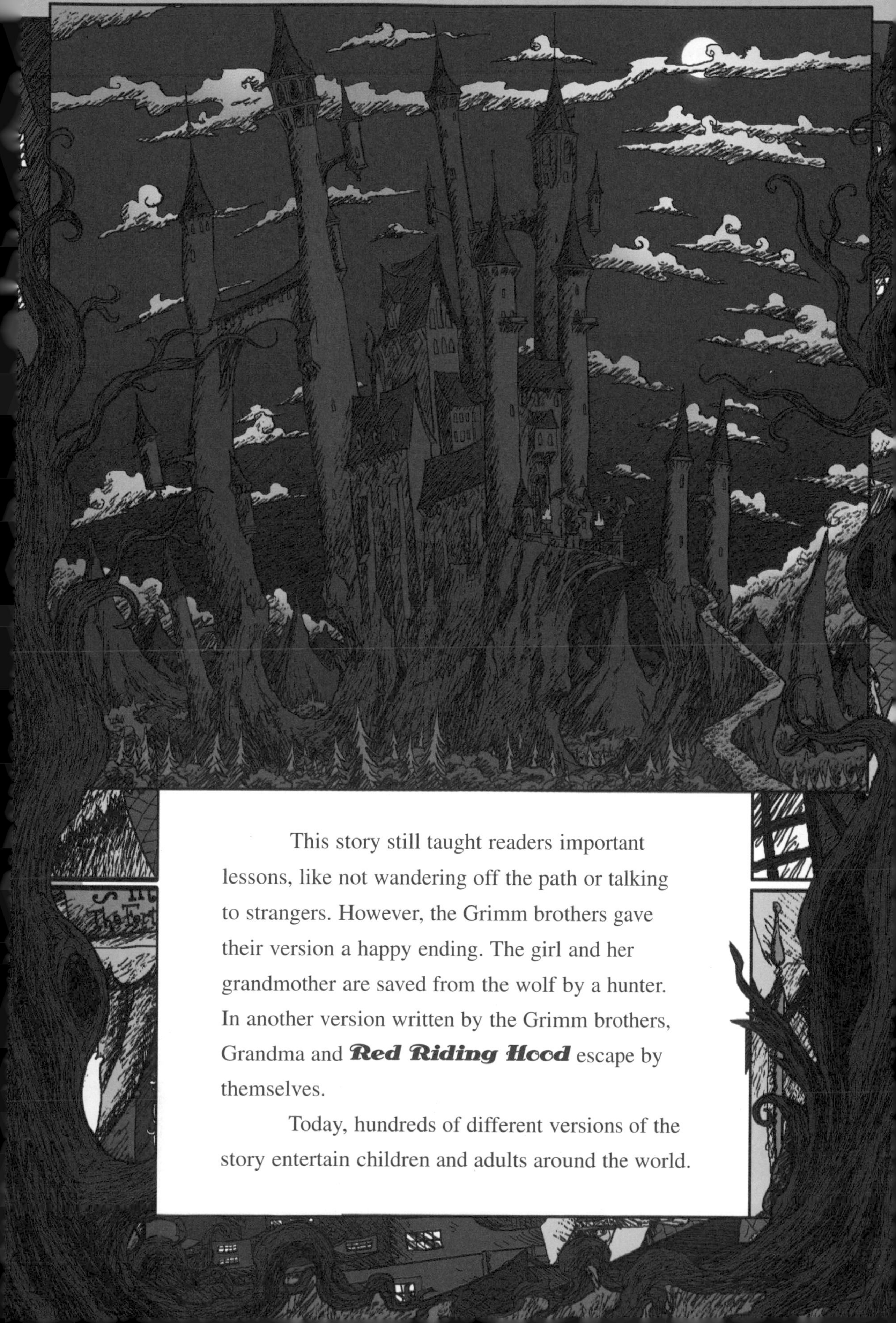

This story still taught readers important lessons, like not wandering off the path or talking to strangers. However, the Grimm brothers gave their version a happy ending. The girl and her grandmother are saved from the wolf by a hunter. In another version written by the Grimm brothers, Grandma and **Red Riding Hood** escape by themselves.

Today, hundreds of different versions of the story entertain children and adults around the world.

# Discussion Questions

1. Why do you think Ruby trusted the wolf? What could she have done differently to keep herself safe?

2. At the end of the story, Ruby has to harm the wolf in order to save herself. Do you think this decision was okay? Why or why not?

3. Fairy tales are often told over and over again. Have you heard the Little Red Riding Hood fairy tale before? How is this version of the story different from other versions you've heard, seen, or read?

# Writing Prompts

1. Fairy tales are fantasy stories, often about wizards, goblins, giants, and fairies. Many fairy tales have a happy ending. Write your own fairy tale. Then, read it to a friend or family member.

2. In this book, Ruby has a couple of good luck charms, including her red riding hood and a four-leaf clover. Do you have any good luck charms? Write about the object and why it's lucky.

3. Imagine you were being chased through a forest by the big, bad wolf. What would you do? Write a story about how you would get away and survive.

# Internet Sites

The book may be over, but the adventure is just beginning.

Do you want to read more about the subjects or ideas in this book? Want to play cool games or watch videos about the authors who write these books? Then go to FactHound. At *www.facthound.com*, you'll be able to do all that, and more. The FactHound website can also send you to other safe Internet sites.

## Check it out!